This one's for Shane McKenzie: a great writer and an even better friend.

Madness Heart Press
2006 Idlewilde Run Dr.
Austin, Texas 78744

Cover by Jim Agpalza

First Edition
www.madnessheart.press

Acknowledgments

This book would not have been possible without two crucial conversations. The first took place between J. David Osborne, Kelby Losack, and me a few years ago. It focused on the ritual nature of wrestling matches and asked what might happen if a promotion as large as the WWE had used black magic to attain its wealth and status. Was there a match in particular we could point to as the definitive turning point? Who would be affected, and what would they do if they could reset things? We agreed that the submission match between Bret Hart and Steve Austin at WrestleMania 13 had all the elements necessary, including the deliberate spillage of blood, and not long after that bout, WWE became a publicly traded, billion-dollar company. I'm not a conspiracy theorist, but it's fun to speculate, especially within the confines of fiction.

The second conversation was between John Baltisberger at Madness Heart Press and me. We discussed how "sports stories" were once a staple of the old pulps and classic horror comics but have since faded from the arena of genre fiction, not including romance, which has plenty of sports-themed books of varying heat levels.

For classic examples, I can point to Robert E. Howard's boxing stories and a grisly comic where a famous quarterback uses footballs stitched in human flesh to throw game-winning passes all season long (I wish I could remember what that one's called). Those are just two, and I urge interested readers to check out the Pulp Fiction Archive or luminist.org for more. Bottom line: John and I agreed that I should write one of these stories for him. Even though it's technically not a sport, we decided on a professional wrestling theme because it's the closest thing to a sport I know anything about.

I'd also like to thank Lisa Lee Tone for her tireless support as an editor and friend, Jim Agpalza for Bladejob's deliciously gruesome cover, Jeff Burk who cohosts Make Your Own Damn Podcast with me, Judith Sonnet for her infectious enthusiasm, everyone I met at the Ghoulish Book Festival, the KillerCon family, Aron Beauregard and Daniel Volpe for their extremely kind blurbs, Stephen Cooper for his awesome YouTube channel showcasing all the badasses who make up this current wave of splatterpunk and extreme horror, A.E. Padilla, the good people at Scares That Care, and all my collaborators on past, present, and future works.

Last but most importantly, I'm sending love to my family, namely: Jean and the kids, my brother and parents, and the Morrises.

Writing a story is, like all things, a holistic process. Everyone named here, and probably some who aren't, has helped write this book and others without typing a single word, and I'm forever grateful for them.

Lucas Mangum
Somewhere in Central, TX
5/2/2023

BLADEJOB

LUCAS MANGUM

A Madness Heart Press Publication

1

The bus stopped at the intersection of Farm to Market Road 783 and a dirt road named Gunnar Path. The road signs were faded on their faces and rusty at their corners. Brian Hearns stood, hardly fazed by the creak of his joints, and shouldered his backpack. Because he'd still maintained a good deal of his size while in prison, the other passengers gawked as he passed. He dipped a half-hearted nod at the bus driver when he reached the front, then stepped off the vehicle. He took a deep breath, deep enough to taste as well as smell the air. It was dusty with a hint of cedar but otherwise differed little, if at all, from the air in the prison yard.

The bus engine rumbled as it accelerated and drove down the paved F.M. 783, leaving Brian standing in its dust. Once it faded from sight, Brian turned toward Gunnar Path. The road stretched beyond the horizon. Feather reeds and cacti stood on either side of its entrance like gathered wrestlers in extravagant ring attire. He knew all about that.

More foliage stretched for countless acres further back from the road. It obscured all signs of civilization aside from Gunnar Path itself, which made the road seem out of place, here either by accident or by some cruel joke. Somewhere beyond it all stood his new home.

As the bus engine faded in the distance, Brian started down Gunnar Path, sticking to the side of the gravel road. He passed fences, some made of planks, some constructed with barb wire. Rusty mailboxes signaled houses; most of them were receded from the road with big yards out in front. A few had horses. One had a medium-sized dog that yipped gleefully when it spotted him. The place should've been a paradise.

He walked on, breathing more dust and cedar. The backpack was light, and he was strong, but after a while, it made his shoulders ache. A mile and a half in, he spotted the address his lawyer gave him on one of the boxes.

The concrete driveway lay behind an open aluminum gate. A black GMC Suburban had somehow gotten on the property and was parked just outside the two-car garage. He stopped to examine it from a distance. Its windows were tinted. When he made his approach, he never took his eyes from it. As he got closer, the driver's door opened, and a man in a black suit got out. He wore shades and didn't acknowledge Brian at all. Brian wondered if he could take the guy if he meant trouble. Once upon a time, he would've had little doubt. They were about the same build, but the suit had youth on his side. Still not looking at Brian, he walked to the back driver's side door and opened it. A woman stepped out wearing a black skirt and matching jacket.

Though twenty-five years had passed, Brian recognized his former boss's daughter immediately. Some faces were impossible to forget.

Reagan McLaughlin followed the driver to the back of the SUV. He opened the hatch, and Reagan reached inside. She pulled out a black box and carried it toward Brian. It was as big as a medium-sized cooler, large enough that she would've been better suited using a dolly to transport it, but she hugged it to herself like it contained something precious.

The driver closed the hatch and stood watching her approach. He might have been watching Brian too, but the shades made it hard to tell. Reagan stopped six or seven paces away from Brian and smirked at him. Her eyes were bright, even brighter than he remembered.

He wondered if it was natural, or if she had simply put in enhancers.

"I bet you're glad to be out," she said.

He looked at his new house. It was ranch-sized and had a log exterior. An immaculate lawn made a perfect rectangle around the structure. It looked like home—it should've felt like home—but he perceived it like a dream image or a frame from a film. There was a tangible, though not quite visible, distance between him and the abode, no matter how close he physically stood to it.

"I'm not sure yet," he said.

Her smile broadened, but she showed no teeth. She adjusted her grip on the box. A muscle worked in her jaw. The box had some serious weight. The Reagan McLaughlin Brian knew would never carry such a burden herself. Twenty-five years could change a person, at least in the fast-moving outside world. While incarcerated, Brian had the same routine. He ate, crapped, and read. Sometimes, he slept and worked out. Aside his hair going gray and some flab buildup around his midsection, Brian was the same man, the same broken man, even though the world had moved on.

"Are you gonna let me inside?" Reagan asked.

He looked from her face to the box to the suited driver. Brian nodded at her, and she nodded at the driver. The driver got back into the GMC. Reagan followed Brian to the door of his new house. He keyed in the code on the lockbox and took out the house key. He slid the key into the door and cast another glance at Reagan.

Her smile had faded, giving way to a stony expression. Even as she'd put on a little weight over the years and faced the same challenges from gravity all people did, her face had retained much of the sharp, angular qualities it possessed in her youth. Her eyes were sharpest of all. He'd never understood the expression "staring daggers" until the day he met her. She didn't have to be mad to do it either. It was just something she did. These daggers were surgical, scalpels meant for dissection, for revealing secrets printed on the hidden parts of oneself. And speaking of hidden …

"Why are you here?" Brian asked.

"I'm here to help, Brian." She exchanged her stony expression for one of mock offense, but the change didn't last. She tilted her head toward the door and gestured with the box. "Let me in. I'll explain everything."

They went inside. Their footsteps made hollow

knocks on the hardwood. The place had an earthy smell that wouldn't have been out of place inside a cabin in the woods. All the furniture was at least a decade old, not that it mattered to him. He hadn't seen the inside of a house since the late nineties. Everything looked new, but none of it looked like home.

"I'll put this down here," Reagan said, carrying the box to a cherrywood coffee table.

"What is that thing?" he asked.

The box sounded heavy when she set it down. It wasn't cardboard. He could see his reflection in it. Reagan sat on the couch and folded her hands over her crossed legs. Her skirt rode up, showing a generous amount of thigh. She'd always been a looker, and she'd aged nicely, not that he had any interest. After what happened to land him behind bars, he doubted he'd ever want sex again. Instead, he merely observed her attributes the way a clinician might appreciate a healthy specimen.

"It was a long walk from the bus stop," she said, as if he didn't know that. He glanced up from her leg and met her gaze. If she'd caught him looking, she seemed unaffected. "You must be exhausted."

"That's an understatement," he said. "And not just from the walk either."

"It's been a hard quarter century."

"Yes, ma'am."

She tilted back her head and laughed out loud. It sounded put-on but not even properly faked, as if she didn't understand the concept. "Ma'am?" she asked. "Come on."

"Sorry. Reagan."

She gestured to an armchair. "Have a seat. We have a lot to discuss."

"We do?"

She flashed that smirk again. Brian unslung his backpack and sat. Two and a half decades worth of fatigue settled into every muscle. He could've fallen asleep without the company. Maybe even with it. Reagan leaned back and steepled her fingers.

"I'll cut right to the chase, Brian. I know you didn't kill that *woman*."

She sneered on the word *woman* as if she hated to think of the deceased as anything like her. *She* was a woman, a human being. The dead thing from Brian's hotel room all those years ago was something less, born for victimhood, but not to him.

"Starlite," Brian breathed. "*Vanessa*."

"Vanessa. Sure." The stony expression returned. "Whatever her name, I know you're innocent."

He searched inward. Memories of clawed hands and mass quantities of blood flooded his mind's eye. Words he'd spoken so many times that he now believed them, regardless of what he remembered, reached his lips.

"I don't remember killing her, but I must have. I was the only one there. I'd do anything to set things right, but it's too late."

"Is it?" she asked.

Her question and the playful tone in which she asked it set fire to his blood. He slammed a fist on the chair's arm and leaned forward. He put his hands on his knees and glared at Reagan.

"Why are you here? If it's to talk in riddles, you can go back out to your FBI agent and his gas guzzler. It's been a long fucking day, and I'd like to get so drunk I don't know what year it is, which, after all this time, wouldn't be so hard."

"Right," she said, unfazed by his outburst. "Let's cut to the chase."

She put a hand on top of the black box.

"What is that thing?"

"It's a gift," she said. Brian opened his mouth to protest her coyness again, but she held up a disarming hand. "And that's not a riddle. Let's see if this sounds familiar: Brian "Bad Guy" Hearns, three-time world champion and probably the hardest worker in the biz, carried my father's All-American Professional Wrestling during the mid-nineties downturn but never quite reached the heights of someone like Invincible Vincent James."

"Fuck that guy, and fuck you for mentioning him."

She raised her eyebrows and stared at him a beat.

"Are you going to let me finish?" she asked.

He forced himself to breathe.

"Sorry. Continue."

"The business was all set to change, though, after Brian Hearns, who, despite his moniker, had been a good guy his entire career, turned heel. The heel turn had been brewing for months, and it wasn't at all unjustified. It seemed that both behind the camera and in front of the camera, the poor Bad Guy kept getting screwed at every opportunity. It all came, quite literally, to a bloody head at *Superslam 13*."

Reagan paused to assess Brian's state. As he watched her speak, he clenched and unclenched his fist. His skin got hot and uncomfortable with every word she spoke. Her eyes held a knowing twinkle. She was getting to him.

"That bloody head belonged to Redneck Miller, and after he passed out in your Dead to Rights submission hold, you beat on him some more, cementing your turn to the dark side. It ushered in a new era for AAPW. A bloodier, edgier one that skyrocketed the promotion into the stratosphere of the entertainment industry. Does that sound about right?"

He clenched his teeth. It'd give him a headache later, but it was all that kept him from screaming. Someone else was screaming, though, deep in the shaded alley of his memory. Reagan's smirk returned.

"You were supposed to be there for its ascent too." She sighed, sounding like a mother disappointed in her child, even though she was nearly twenty years his junior. "Unfortunately, things didn't go according to plan."

"I had habits," Brian said.

"Everyone has habits," Reagan said. "But your habits couldn't predict what happened that night. You didn't kill that woman. The Agents killed her."

Again, memories of those creatures and all that blood flickered through his mind's eye.

"Agents?" he asked, even though he was reasonably sure he would dread her answer.

"They feed on blood and do the work necessary to ensure the goals of the ritual are achieved."

He zeroed in on one word. It was a word that carried

so much weight to some but, until that night, had carried none for him. Ever the realist, he had discounted every bizarre thing he heard as the product of mental illness at best or charlatanism at worst. All that changed the night Starlite died, but he couldn't allow himself to think about that, lest his mind slip away.

"What ritual?"

"Do you really think my father and his company reached its heights through hard work and dumb luck?"

"So, what? He made a deal with the devil?"

She rolled her eyes and made a disgusted chuff. "You would see things in such simplistic terms."

"Why are you here, Reagan?"

He'd injected all the hardness he could muster into his voice. He'd sat up straight and glared at her. It would've shaken anyone, man and woman alike, but not Reagan. She ran her hand along the smooth surface of the black box and stared at it with an absent expression. It reminded him of someone checking a car's paintjob for imperfections too small to see. When she looked at Brian again, her jaw went hard and her eyes darkened.

"I'm offering you your life back," she said. "Rituals can be undone. It only takes another ritual. I'd do it myself, but …" She looked off to the side and stuck out her lip. "I'm tainted."

"I'm no virgin either," Brian said. Again, memories of what put him behind bars threatened to surface. "Obviously."

"I'm not talking about sexual purity," she said, her voice sharpened. "Where do you think Daddy learned about black magic?"

"You?"

"Ding-ding-ding!" She grinned wide when she did that and looked half-crazy, like a clown trying to keep it up after packing too many birthday parties into one afternoon. When the grin disappeared, she scooted to the end of the sofa and leaned on its arm to stare at Brian. "You win the chance to take back your life. It's all in that box: what to do, how to do it, and why you absolutely should."

Brian looked from the box to her. He glanced around the cozy but alien interior of his house. It stood a good bit away from his neighbors and far from civilization, but also far from family and friends. He'd gone from one prison to another.

"Why do you want this?" he asked. "Aren't you a billionaire or something?"

"Money isn't everything," she said. "Maybe I'm

bored."

Her face darkened, a stark contrast to her off-hand remarks.

"Is that it?" Brian asked.

She looked out the window. The GMC sat idling in the driveway. The driver could've been doing anything behind the tinted windows. Brian couldn't imagine how anyone who had a chauffeur could be unhappy enough to undo a timeline, not that such a thing was even possible.

"How do I know you're even telling the truth?" he asked.

"You don't," she said with a shrug, still looking outside. "But what do you have to lose? Give some blood. Say some words. Worst case scenario, nothing happens and you live the rest of your life alone in your little cabin."

Brian put his hands on his knees and stood. The joints cracked in protest.

"I'm sorry you came all the way out here," he said. "But I'm supposed to see my daughter tomorrow. I'd like to relax a little and get used to my surroundings before then. Shit isn't bound to be perfect, but I think I'd rather rebuild the old-fashioned way."

"A day at a time, huh? Kind of goes against the *drink*

until I forget what year it is plan."

"We're complex creatures, even us wrestlers."

"I doubt that," Reagan said, standing and smoothing her skirt. "I'm not all that hard to figure out. I don't imagine you're any different."

"It was nice to see you, Reagan." He held out his hand for her to shake it. She took it. "Give my best to the old man."

As they shook, her lips made a tight, joyless smile. She released his hand and headed for the door.

"Don't forget your box," Brian said.

Some of her initial spirit flickered back into her expression.

"Why don't you hold on to it? You might change your mind."

He walked her to the door and locked it behind her. He looked at the box, sitting like a monolith on the antique coffee table.

"Doubtful," he said. He dug the phone his attorney had shown him how to use out of the bag and typed a message to Genevieve, asking if they were still on for breakfast the next day. He found the liquor cabinet and poured himself three fingers of something Japanese.

Before—

Brian Hearns did another rail of cocaine off the ass of a woman who called herself Starlite. She giggled as he squeezed her buttocks. He closed his eyes and let the tingle of the drug work its way through his nasal cavity. She spun out of his grasp and rose to tickle him. He opened his eyes and gave her a light shove. She stared at him in what he thought was mock hurt, but in the room's dimness, he couldn't tell for sure.

"I didn't push too hard, did I?" he asked.

"No," she said and shook her head. "I'd let you know if you hurt me."

"Good," he said. "Turn over."

"Another line?" she asked.

"Yes," he said. "I can still feel feelings."

"Anyone ever tell you you're screwed up in the

head?"

"All the time. Now, turn over."

She rolled her eyes and smirked but lay on her belly with her legs straight. He mused as he laid out another fat line that he and Starlite weren't so different from each other. They both used their bodies to tell stories, and they both had scars.

"I just don't get it," she said.

"Don't get what?"

"Why you're so keen on self-destructing. After your match with Miller tonight, things are looking up, aren't they?"

"Maybe not," he said, bending to do the line.

"How do you figure?"

He paused inches from her ass cheek.

"I'm a villain now. Yeah, maybe it will draw money, and yeah, Miller deserves the push, but …" He grimaced and tried to think how to articulate himself. The fat line of coke and the promise of oblivion lured him away from finding the words. "It's not important," he said. "And I don't really want to talk about it."

Before she could protest, Brian snorted the whole line in one go and snapped his head back. The numbness spread across his face like oil across a hot pan. He grabbed the backs of her thighs and squeezed.

"Goddamn!" he said.

Starlite looked over her shoulder. "Now, are you going do me like you paid for, or am I gonna have to call the ambulance when your dumb ass ODs?"

He grumbled and grabbed hold of her hips with his meaty palms, pulling her to her hands and knees. He considered undoing his pants and thrusting into her. He'd taken her from behind before and knew from the months he'd gotten to know her that it was the quickest way to get her off. Instead, he turned and slid face-up underneath her.

"Sit," he said.

That brought another giggle from her. At least she was playing along, taking the hint that he didn't want to talk. She lowered herself onto his mouth and lightly ground against him, brushing her shaved pubis across his lips and nose. She smelled like vanilla and cherries, obviously perfume.

"No," he said. "Hold still."

"Okay," she said with a sigh.

"What are you complaining about? I'm doing all the work."

"If you say so. Mind if I smoke while you go at it?"

"Go right ahead."

He hated cigarettes. He hated everything from the

way they smelled, to how they made other people smell, to how they'd killed some wrestlers from back in the day that he'd called mentors and brothers. It drove him nuts that Starlite smoked, and he occasionally considered telling her not to puff away when he was paying for the time with her. He couldn't imagine her job was easy, though. Even if it seemed as though she liked him—they always planned to see each other months in advance, and she always gave him an extra half-hour on the house—he was, at the end of the day, just a customer. And customers *used* the products they purchased; he was *using* her, even though he sometimes thought he loved her.

Starlite grabbed a pack of Pall Malls from the nightstand, rocked to a kneeling position over his face, and lit up. If she wanted, she easily could've smothered him with her pussy. Even with the business on its way up again and all the money that would bring, he wouldn't try to stop her. He could imagine no death so sweet.

He licked at her folds and gently kissed between them. He found her clit and sucked on it. She began to moan. Her juices drizzled away the flavor of her perfume. He preferred her natural taste, this salty-sweet essence that made him drunk with lust.

Starlite reached behind her with her free hand and grabbed his shaft. As she stroked and smoked and rocked her hips, he could hardly believe the talent of this woman. It brought new meaning to the term *multitasking*, and she made it look so easy.

They came together, and she tightened her thighs and sat all the way down on his face like she'd read his mind, like she aimed to grant his secret wish.

But why is she screaming?

And there's something wrong with how she's squirming …

Oh, God, no. Please, not again.

Something muffled her screams. He shimmied out from under her. Vaginal juices still coated his mouth and chin like a mucilaginous beard. His own spunk ran in rivulets down his abs and dripped onto the crumpled sheets.

"What the hell?" he sputtered, twirling into a plank position.

Starlite flailed her arms and staggered back. She tried to stand but got her feet caught in the comforter and spilled over the side of the bed. The wall above the headboard had turned pale and fleshy. It had pores and even a light layer of hair. A wet, ragged slit glistened like a fresh evisceration done by a hand that couldn't cut straight. Something red and sinewy lined the hole's insides. The opening led to impossible black, a black beyond black. And it wasn't empty.

On the floor, Starlite tussled with something gray and scaly. It had small but grotesquely muscular limbs like a 'roided up baby. Its bulbous head bore a series of plates stretching from between its eyes to the occipital knob. They were lined with tiny horns like dog teeth. It was otherwise toad-faced, with bulging yellow eyes and gaping nostrils. Jagged brown teeth filled its impossibly wide mouth.

It snapped at her and lapped at her with a green tongue. Its claws slashed at her. She held it at bay but wouldn't be able to for long. It attacked with the ferocity of a rabid wolverine and had already made weepy crimson scrapes on her arms, breasts, and cheeks. Some of the wounds looked deep and offered glimpses of the meat beneath Starlite's flesh.

"Oh, Jesus Christ," Brian whimpered, hating the unmanly tremble in his voice.

Starlite's head whipped around, and she cast a crazy-eyed expression Brian's way.

"Fucking help me!" she shrieked.

He blinked away his panic. Glanced from the creature to the hole in the wall to Starlite's face, which was now red with exertion. He got a running start and rammed his foot into the creature's belly. The blow connected, and even with his drug-addled body, it came with tremendous force. His target flew out of Starlite's grasp and arced across the room. It landed hard on the carpet and rolled until it thumped against the door.

Hardly fazed, the creature scrambled to its feet and reached out with its clawed hands. With a shrill gurgle, it charged Brian and Starlite like a demonic child running in for a hug and lunged at Brian's Chicago girl, claws flailing. Starlite caught it and hoisted it over her head to hurl it across the room, but its hands and feet tangled in her hair. She cried out, twisted her ankle, and fell again. This time, her head struck the nightstand.

Brian moved to pull the creature off her, but a series of squelching sounds from the hole in the wall drew his attention. More of the things, fucking *imps*, were crawling out of the gristly opening, hissing and gurgling. They were a tangle of limbs, a swarm of yellow eyes and gnashing teeth. Brian put up his fists to defend himself, but they ignored him.

Instead, they dogpiled the fallen Starlite.

Her consciousness returned when the first set of razor teeth clamped on her forearm, and she screamed, thrashing and kicking. But there were too many of them, at least half a dozen. She was gasping something. It sounded like *God*. He wanted to help her, but his feet had locked into place. He wanted God to help her, but no miracles graced the walls of hotel rooms where prostitutes met middle-aged wrestlers for a roll in the hay.

His bladder felt set to burst. A voice in his head screamed for him to do something, but he couldn't heed its command. Starlite screamed for God again. Or no, she was saying something else. The word broke through the mental fog of panic and became clear. She was saying *gun*.

He shook himself from his trance of helplessness. "Where is it?" he cried.

"Get my gun!"

He didn't understand. He hadn't seen a gun.

New wounds opened on her every second, throwing flecks of blood against the carpet, the walls, and Brian's feet. The flesh came away as easily as wet paper.

Brian's gaze darted about the room until it landed on Starlite's leather purse. He scrambled for it. Dumped its contents onto the bed. Swiped the gun and pointed it at … He couldn't decide what to shoot. He worried he'd accidentally hit her, even as the creatures slashed open newer, deeper wounds.

One of them had taken a chunk out of her shoulder and chewed on the gristle it pulled free. Another had bitten off her ear, and the blood soaked the entire left side of her head, turning her blond hair dark red. He aimed the gun at one of the imps and squeezed the trigger.

Click.

Fuck. Safety.

A gout of crimson sprayed across the room and splattered his face. The warmth of it, the metallic taste of it, awakened a beast in him the way her pussy juices had so recently. But these were different juices, and they made him a different beast.

He cried out and charged for the feeding frenzy. He swung the gun wildly, smacking away creature after creature. They were hard-bodied little fuckers, but they tumbled off their victim and gathered like a swarm of wasps onto the bed. One turned and gave him the middle finger, a gesture which sent another blaze of fury through his veins.

He managed to find and click off the safety. He didn't stop firing, even after the hole resealed itself. When the police and the hotel manager burst into the room several minutes later, they found a bloody, naked Bad Guy Brian Hearns standing with an empty gun over the bloody, naked, and very dead Vanessa Carter, known to her clients as Starlite.

Now—

As the memory washed through his mind, Brian could smell and taste her blood. A palpable panic surged through him as it had surged through him that night. It clenched every muscle in his body. He broke out in a sweat so heavy it soaked his T-shirt in a matter of seconds, and he curled into a ball on the couch, still clutching the glass of whiskey like a talisman. Starlite's screams were so loud, they could've been in the room with him now. It defied the passage of time and the distance from Chicago to Central Texas. Over the time he'd spent in prison, the memories grew less vivid and less frequent, but the intensity of this current episode reminded him of the early days.

He downed the rest of his glass in one pull and stared at the liquor cabinet the way a homeless man in the winter might stare at a heated shelter. He wanted more booze and a lot of it. Perhaps if he upended the bottle in his mouth, he could forget all the awful shit that had happened to him—awful shit that felt like it was still happening right now—but even with the promise of intoxicated relief, he couldn't pull himself off the couch. It felt like a large fist had clamped itself around his body.

Out of the corner of his eye, he spotted a flash of something gray and sinewy scurrying across the room. They had come, those fucking imps—*Agents*, Reagan called them. They'd waited for him to get out of prison, and now they would eat his eyeballs, his throat, his heart.

He closed his eyes and breathed deep. He counted to ten, then to twenty.

The tension still gripped him in its giant, unforgiving fist. It could have crushed him and ended his suffering but was simply satisfied letting him know it could. He still tasted Starlite's blood and felt the crippling helplessness he'd felt as he watched her get rent apart.

He opened his eyes, and with a scream, he broke from the grip of the unseen hand and hurled the empty glass at the wall. It shattered, and some of the panic subsided. He scanned the room for signs of imps. Finding none, he dared to put his feet on the ground and stand. The tension left his muscles, but echoes of it pulsed through him, an unkind reminder it had been there and would more than likely come again.

Maybe he couldn't have loved Starlite, but he'd

loved how she made him feel. With her, he'd felt like he was worth something. Even though his heel turn had promised success, it also signaled a looming end to his career. He would no longer be the torchbearer for AAPW. Women like Starlite (and Brooklynn in Brooklyn and Lolita in Nashville and Sapphire in Waco) had made him feel like he still had it, whatever *it* was.

That was a long time ago. What did he have now, beyond traumatic memories?

He checked his phone for a reply from Genevieve. She hadn't replied yet, but a small note next to the message indicated it had been read. His thumb hovered over the key as he contemplated a follow-up message. Instead, he put the phone back down and cast a wary glance at the black box. His shadowy reflection stared back.

3

Despite Brian's agitation, the softness of his new bed managed to lull him to sleep. It was worlds away from the seemingly concrete cot in his cell. His final thought as he lay in the dark was a hopeful one. Tomorrow he would see his daughter face-to-face. The last time he'd seen her, she was little more than a toddler. His ex-wife had never brought Genevieve to see him in prison. As she got older, Genevieve had never come of her own accord. Perhaps tomorrow would be a true new chapter. An imperfect one, maybe, but beautiful in its own way.

When he woke up the next morning, a message notification blinked on his phone. He swiped the phone from the nightstand and sat up to read it.

Dad, I'm glad to hear your out of prison and getting settled into your new house. Whether or not you're innocent,

I can't imagine the past twenty-some-odd years have been easy. I've talked things over with Chris—her husband—and Ruthanne—her therapist—and I've decided not to see you tomorrow. I think it might be too triggering for me.

I realize this isn't what you want or need to hear, but I need to think about me.

I hope you come to understand. And I don't want you to think I don't love you.

It's just hard.

Sorry.

Brian tapped the reply box and let his thumb linger over the keyboard. Several possible responses ran through his mind, none of them charitable.

No problem, I understand. I guess.

What the hell? Really?

Can't you at least try?

Did your fucking mother put you up to this?

He typed none of these things. The urge to hurl his phone across the room as he'd thrown the empty glass the previous night came and went. He set it back down on the nightstand instead. He lay back down and shut his eyes. It was restless darkness, full of writhing white worms and scattered, glimmering spots outlined by bizarre colors he couldn't name. He snapped his eyes open a couple seconds later. A long way past falling back asleep, he flung off the blanket and tromped out of the bedroom.

On his way to the kitchen, he looked at the black box. From a distance, his reflection looked amorphous, a mere blob moving across the box's smooth surface like a cancerous ghost.

As he entered the kitchen and found the coffeemaker, he felt the box's presence. It itched at the base of his skull. When he reached back to scratch it, the itch moved further inward, irritating some untouchable place inside. Only splitting his skull open could give him the relief he craved.

He filled the coffeemaker with water and put a filter full of grinds into the basket. Still, his brain itched, and with the sensation, Reagan's voice spoke up, a whisper against his ear, repeating her words from the previous day.

You win the chance to take back your life. It's all in that box: what to do, how to do it, and why you absolutely should.

He closed the lid and hit the brew button. The coffee smelled expensive. His lawyer's team had gone out of their way to make his readjustment to life on the outside as comfortable as possible.

Still, the prickling in his brain. Still, Reagan's disembodied whispers. He could almost feel her hot breath as she spoke, even though when he looked, he found no one standing in the kitchen with him.

But what do you have to lose?

Give some blood. Say some words.

Worst case scenario, nothing happens.

You live the rest of your life alone in your little cabin.

His reasons for turning her away had seemed so right.

I'm supposed to see my daughter tomorrow.

Genevieve.

Her heartbreaking response undid it all.

Might be too triggering. Hope you come to understand.

The coffee made a wet purr when it finished brewing. He poured himself a mug and sat in front of the black box. His reflection stared back at him with an expression made unreadable by shadows. He set down the coffee without sipping it and opened the box by undoing three brass clasps. A dusty, dank smell wafted from beneath the lid. He made a groan of disgust and cringed away from the offensive odor.

What the hell did you put in there?

Reagan's words, *A gift …*

"Some gift."

He put his hand over his mouth and nose and leaned forward to peer inside the box. The sight was worse than the smell. The box was full of bones. Desiccated limbs were piled atop each other underneath a hollow ribcage. A grinning skull sat atop it all. Its black eye sockets seemed to stare up at Brian, though the eyes themselves had long ago gone to dust.

Some gift indeed.

"The fuck am I supposed to do with you?"

In one of the skeletal hands, he spotted a folded sheet of … something. It looked like parchment or leather. He reached inside even as he inwardly screamed at himself to do anything but. His hand brushed the dry fingerbones, and his chest clenched. Was he really doing this? He freed the parchment with a papery rustle and lifted it out of the box. It felt like animal skin, but he cast a wary glance at the piled bones and prayed that was all it was.

I feel ridiculous.

Nonetheless, he unfolded the parchment. A message was written on it with big letters in dark ink.

My name is Richard. I'm here to help. Say my name to wake me up.

"Richard, huh?"

He scoffed and tossed the parchment back into the box.

What am I even doing?

Reagan must have been playing a fucked-up joke. If there was a punchline, though, it was lost on him. There was no way to reset timelines. Skeletons didn't talk. Imps or Agents or whatever they called themselves weren't real. Brian Hearns had really killed Starlite. Vanessa Carter, a mother of three who'd taken up the world's oldest profession to help herself through a difficult time for her family. She'd stuck with it because she was good at it and it was easy. And Brian had killed her, taken a mother away from her kids. He was the only real demon here.

He put both hands on the lid and began to push it closed. Something inside held it open. Brian pushed away from the table and cocked his head like a confused dog. One of the skeleton arms was raised, now attached to the hand. Its fingers were splayed against the box's lid.

"No fucking way," he said, but he trusted his eyes. They hadn't deceived him the night of Starlite's death, and they weren't deceiving him now.

The lid lifted. The skeletal limb rose, picking up other pieces like a magnet grabbing paperclips. Brian watched with a gaping mouth as the skeleton assembled itself. It came together as if by unseen hands until it stood, headless, in the box. Brian looked the nearly complete figure up and down. His mouth tried to form words, but all his spit had dried up and he'd forgotten how to speak.

The skull levitated from the box. Something dark purple glimmered in its cavernous eye sockets as it rose. It hovered over the space between the skeleton's shoulders and lowered itself, attaching to the spine with a final click.

Fully formed, the skeleton stepped out of the box and down from the table. Its feet clacked against the hardwood. Face-to-face with Brian, it opened its jaws. More of that purple light glowed within.

"Hello, Brian," it said.

The voice warbled and cracked like a bad radio signal. It sounded both impossibly far away and uncomfortably close, all at once. It could have been multiple voices, two or three layered atop each other like some backwards-masked, satanic recording.

The skeleton stood only a few inches away. It was like some twisted parody of a stare-down before a wrestling match. The purple light in the eye sockets pulsed, expanding and contracting like ethereal hearts. Up close like this, the scent of dust and decay was nearly oppressive, a cloud of suffocating death. Brian remained in place, not out of bravado or even crippling disbelief. He stayed because he needed to see what would happen next, how this crazy-ass scenario would play out.

The skeleton put out its hand. "Pleased to meet you," it said. "I love your work."

Brian looked down at the hand and back up at the skeleton's face.

"I'm not shaking a dead man's hand."

"Perhaps that's wise." It lowered its hand. "My name is Richard Kyle. I'm here to help."

Brian recalled Reagan's words. She hadn't said anything about a dead man in a box. The name Richard Kyle did sound familiar, though. A common name, sure, but it was more than that, something from the distant, pre-ritual past.

"How do you plan on doing that?"

"It's better if I show you," Richard said. "You need to see the past, when and how the first ritual took place. That way, you'll know which moments need undoing."

The gravity of what they were discussing seemed so unreal. He heard Richard's words from both immediate proximity and a great distance, and it wasn't just the way they sounded. It felt more like he was learning the rules of a game than something with real-world implications. He wanted to both dissociate and be present. His consciousness couldn't decide which to do, so it did both, which made things even more disorienting.

"If you say so, bone man," he said, the unreality of the moment inspiring bravado. "You gonna put it on the TV or something?"

"Not quite."

Brian narrowed his eyes as Richard turned on creaky joints and reached into the box. He pulled out the piece of parchment Brian had tossed in and held it up.

"It's the last piece of my skin," he said. Brian instinctively rubbed his hand on his pants. "Preserved for this moment." Richard held out the dried flap of flesh. "Eat."

Brian scoffed. "Fuck no. You just told me it was your skin."

"It's no different than your holy communion."

"I'm not Catholic," Brian said with a smirk. "Not anymore, anyway."

"Regardless, if you wish to have a second chance, you must eat."

Brian looked from the dry and crinkly shred in the skeleton fingers to the swelling and contracting light in the skeleton's black eye holes. Reagan's words whispered, again as if she'd pressed her lips against his ear.

You win the chance to take back your life.

What do you have to lose?

Brian snatched the shred and put it in his mouth. It moistened on his tongue and grew thicker, more flavorful. It tasted like blood, too much blood. It filled his mouth, a rising sea submerging his tongue and bottom teeth. He gagged as the fluid drizzled down his throat. With a cough, flecks of the blood pattered on his chin.

"Swallow it," Richard said. "Swallow and see."

Every instinct told Brian to spit, but he closed his eyes and gulped down the offensive substance. The darkness behind his eyes lifted to show the night of *Superslam 13.*

4

Before—

While fifty-two-year-old Jack McLaughlin walked the cinderblock hall of the Springtown Horizon, he remembered some words of advice from a dead man.

Once you've thought about doing a ritual, you've already begun it.

If that warning had any truth to it, then Jack had been performing the ritual planned for tonight since his early teenage years. While his father tirelessly contended with the governing body of the nation's wrestling territories, Jack Junior harbored fantasies of buying up all the competition and becoming *the* territory. Once, he'd run the idea past his father and gotten a sore ass for his troubles, but after buying the promotion from the old man, he put his plan into action.

For a while, it looked like it might work. Jack's

All-American Professional Wrestling had become a household name in the mid-1980s, with a closed-circuit showcase that media outlets called "the slam heard 'round the world." It was the third annual *Superslam*, and in the main event, champion Invincible Vincent James performed the impossible, hoisting up the five-hundred-pound Tower of Power and slamming him to the mat in front of a purported ninety-three thousand in attendance and almost one million watching at home. It was a watershed moment for the company and the sport, creating the so-called "wrestling boom."

Jack had used no black magic for any of this either, despite considering it as a very real option more than once. Instead, he'd simply thrown around whatever money he could, raiding talent from the competition until he alone had the best performers the business had to offer. It had made him plenty of enemies, but he was building a legacy, an empire, all while providing for his family and the families of his superstars.

But nothing lasts forever, he thought before knocking on the locker room door.

The door swung open, and Redneck Miller filled its frame. This bruiser came from East Texas. Those who knew him personally said that his character was merely a cranked-up version of his real-life self. He liked to drink beer, work on cars, and go hunting. He also loved the business. Name any wrestler from the sport's storied history, he could rifle off a detailed profile. Give him a date and place, he could say who was on the card and who went over. Redneck Miller would not go over tonight, but it wouldn't matter. He'd be a made man when it was all said and done, even if that was only an added bonus of the ritual.

Now, he eyed up Jack with a combination of respect and suspicion. It was an old school way of thinking, born from a history littered with broken promises and bounced checks.

"Can I come in?" Jack asked.

"You're the boss," Miller said, standing aside.

On the bench, Brian Hearns was lacing up his boots. He stopped and looked up at Jack. His gaze was different from Miller's. There was trust there. Sometimes Jack thought Brian thought of him as a father figure. They'd known each other twenty years, and Brian had given so much to the company. Tonight, he would give even more.

"How're we doing, boys?" Jack asked.

"Upright and breathing," Miller said.

"Just going over everything," Brian said.

Brian Hearns was soft-spoken and meticulous.

Had he not found success in sports entertainment, Jack could've easily seen him going into the arts to become a painter or writer. He just had that demeanor. That wasn't to say he was shy or delicate. He loved interacting with fans—women especially loved him—and his background in amateur wrestling leant a legitimacy to his in-ring work that not everyone on the roster could boast.

"Right," Jack said. "And it's all coming together?"

"You can trust me," Brian said.

Jack looked at Miller, who only nodded.

"Now, listen, guys, I want Miller to get some color tonight."

Both men stared at Jack. All-American Professional Wrestling had a strict "no juicing" policy. Blood was simply not allowed. It could land them in trouble with their sponsors. Jack could tell by their gaping expressions that this was going through both their minds. At least they were loyal.

"Yeah, I know we have our rules," he said, "but I'm asking you to break them. They're my rules, so I trust this won't be a problem. Besides, it's Pay-Per-View. We can get away with it tonight."

"Are you sure?" Miller asked, ever the suspicious one.

"I mean, it will help make him look tougher," Brian said, nodding at Miller and practically answering for Jack. "That's what we want, isn't it?"

"Exactly."

"One problem," Miller said.

A silence fell on the room. It was electric with tension. Jack wondered what Miller would say. He couldn't imagine the bruiser would have any problem shedding blood, certainly not out of fear. Jack had a hard time believing Miller feared much of anything. If not fear, then what? A moral objection? That couldn't be right. Miller loved the business, and wrestling had used blood to heighten drama in matches for decades.

"Well, what is it, pal?" Jack asked.

"Never done it before," Miller said.

Jack looked at Brian. Bad Guy Brian Hearns was a veteran in the business. He knew the ins and outs and everything in between. He'd also never put together a bad match, managing to make even the greenest rookies look like seasoned pros. Jack had relied on him on and off over the last five years to carry the company during a serious low point. It was a low point that would end tonight if only these men could find a way to spill some blood. Brian would have a solution, and he did.

"I could cut him," he said in his nonthreatening,

matter-of-fact way. "I'll be safe."

Jack turned to Miller, trying to gauge how he felt before asking, "Are you okay with that?"

"You won't hurt me?" Miller asked Hearns, surprising Jack with his trepidation.

"You know I'll take care of you."

Jack nodded and clapped both men on the back before Miller had the chance to object.

"All right, so we're doing this?" he asked.

Brian made eye contact with Miller. "You good, Miller?"

"Hell yeah. Let's get some color."

Brian shifted to look at Jack. "All right, we'll do it."

The thing about rituals, the dead man had told Jack, *is not everyone involved needs to know what they're involved in. Not every participant needs to be a* willing *participant. Anyone can be a pawn. Do you understand?*

As far as Jack knew, neither Brian nor Miller believed in magic, black or otherwise. Maybe Miller believed in God. That was a requirement for card-carrying rednecks, Jack thought. Wasn't it? If that were true, he would've outright objected to the spillage of blood, especially his, if he knew it'd be used for some occult purpose. Brian's spirituality, or lack thereof, was more oblique, but Jack strongly doubted he'd be okay participating in a blood ritual, whether he believed in its efficacy or not. Of course, the dead man would have called them fools.

All performances are rituals in a way, he'd said. *Every movie, every concert, every circus, every first date, and, yes, even every wrestling match.*

Not all rituals required blood.

But this one would.

The undercard of *Superslam 13* showcased mostly throwaway matches between reliable, if unexciting, workhorses and impressive looking but green rookies. A three-minute tag-team bout between the Nu-Metalheads and the Hog-Men generated a chorus of boos that would have been thunderous had the building been fuller. A Chicago Street Fight between six of the AAPW's legitimate tough men proved a surprise standout match. The crowd loved the use of two-by-fours, metal trashcans, and fire extinguishers. It was just chaotic enough to cover the men's shortcomings as mat technicians.

Jack McLaughlin wasn't concerned about any of it. His focus lay solely with the semi-main event, the submission match between Redneck Miller and Bad

Guy Brian Hearns. The blood ritual would take place there.

When the Street Fight ended, Jack left the gorilla position before the competitors came through the curtains and headed for the back. He walked the backstage cinderblock hallways until he found the room marked NO ENTRY. He'd written the sign himself on a shred of cardboard in black Sharpie and signed his name at the bottom. Discretion was key, so even though he was the boss, he checked his surroundings for onlookers before opening the door.

Inside, the lighting was dim and crimson-hued. A television played the pay-per-view on mute. It was intermission, and an ad for their next event played on the screen. No matches were yet announced, but they had the logo, the date and time, and the arena. He entered the darkness. Several cloaked figures stood in a circle. Between them burned a thick, black candle, and four smaller candles colored the same. Beneath the candles, Jack's right-hand man, Bruce Peters, had drawn a sigil with charcoal. It was all sharp angles and spiraling curves. In the center, under the black candle, was a crudely sketched shape that could have been a mouth or could have been an anus. Even according to the grimoire Jack had consulted, it was unclear, only that it had to be sketched exactly as shown.

Jack closed the door and found his cloak hanging on the wall beside it. He pulled it over his head, stuck his arms through, and put up the hood. The cloak smelled like a campfire with a hint of old sweat. He approached the circle. The cloaked figures parted so he could join them. He took the hands of the figures beside him. One belonged to Bruce, the other to his daughter Reagan. The other figures were members of his inner circle, two investors, one of the road agents, and the head writer, Johnny D'Amato. Seven total, including Jack himself.

Though Jack had long considered black magic as a means to an end—to be not just the biggest wrestling company in the world but one of the biggest entertainment companies, on par with the likes of Disney—Reagan had introduced him to the dead man. Before that, he'd only entertained it as a fantasy.

Jack McLaughlin had three daughters, all named for Republican presidents. They were Theodora for Roosevelt, Geraldine for Ford, and Reagan for the Great Communicator himself. She was the youngest and the most like her old man. While Theodora had gone on to professorship at Emerson College and Geraldine had joined a hippie commune in Central Pennsylvania, Reagan had inherited her father's mind for business.

Even as a youngster, she'd turned a lemonade stand that would have been a one-weekend endeavor for any other kid into a summer-long operation, even reinvesting her profits into better lemons, better water, more sugar. No other stand in their neighborhood could compete. She even started paying other kids to work the stand for her while she watched from her bedroom window like a construction foreman. Jack had never been so proud.

Now, as Redneck Miller and Bad Guy Brian Hearns made their entrances, Jack squeezed his youngest daughter's hand. It was small but strong. Its palm was cool. Nails like razors tipped its fingers. She had her mother's hands. When her father squeezed her hand, she began to chant. Jack and the others followed suit.

In college, Reagan McLaughlin learned all about black magic. It began with her then-boyfriend, Richard Kyle, an aspiring heavy metal guitarist and singer. He played a record for her by this Norwegian band called Plague Eater and showed her the album artwork. It was loaded with bizarre sigils, elaborate paintings of demons, and lore about gods from the world before humanity came and fucked it all up. Humanity was the plague, and the band (and the deities behind it) would devour the whole race to begin the world anew.

Of course, it was just lore, she'd said, despite feeling her heart flutter with excitement and juicy warmth pulse between her legs. No, Richard had told her. These guys were for real. And Richard planned to get famous using the same magic they had.

Unfortunately for him, Richard Kyle was a complete and irredeemable idiot.

Reagan hadn't started dating him for his brain. She'd pursued him because he was a bleach blond, tanned, ultra-ripped dude with a very sexy, very *manly* singing voice. Despite his lack of higher cognitive functions, he fucked like a stampede. His rebellious nature and fascination with the dark arts made him endlessly fascinating to an upper-class girl like her. He was alien and exciting, the closest thing to one of her dad's neanderthal wrestlers she could find at the University of Connecticut. More than anything else, he made her feel like she was home.

She had him to thank for tonight.

Too bad he'd needed to die to give her what she needed.

She led the chant she learned that night with him in those woods outside South Windsor. After she brought him back to life to tell her how shit had gone wrong.

How he should have performed the ritual rather than the careless way that had gotten his throat torn out.

Poor Richard. At least, in a way, he was still with her.

On the television, the action spilled out of the ring early. Brian Hearns and Redneck Miller exchanged low-blows and whipped each other into the guardrail. Miller took a backdrop onto the concrete floor. Though she could not hear them, she could tell the audience was eating it up. Most stood up from their chairs. Some reached for the tussling performers.

This was all very good. The more intense the energy around the ritual, the better. Her father had said he expected as much from any Brian Hearns match. The man was an artist, Jack often said. Reagan didn't know about that. He was good-looking enough, and his shit looked real, but he always struck her as too much of a do-gooder despite his "Bad Guy" moniker. Good thing he'd be turning heel at the end of the match.

The temperature in the ritual room took a plunge. It felt like someone had opened a window on a January afternoon, though there were no windows and it was almost April. The chanting ceased, but there were other whispers. They came from the shadowed corners and spoke in a language Reagan only knew from one of the samples on the Plague Eater album. It was untranslatable by human tongues. The candlelight blinked from orange to deep blue. Some fog a slightly cooler shade rose from the floor. It swirled around the candles, obscuring the charcoal symbol. An opaque wall of it eclipsed the crimson lights and the flickering television. Tendrils of the stuff enshrouded the feet of the cloaked figures.

"You see this shit, bro?" D'Amato said.

"Johnny," her father grumbled.

Something like spider legs reached from the encircling tendrils, tickling Reagan's ankles and sending chills, not entirely unpleasant, across her flesh. The caresses set her heart aflutter. Her breath caught. She thought she heard the breath of others do likewise. Other things were in the room with them. Everybody knew it.

"I'm Christian," said one of the others. She thought it was Chip, one of her father's investors. "I didn't think we'd be doing this for real."

"It's too late to back out now," she said.

"Like hell it is. I'm out."

"Don't break the circle," her father barked.

Chip whimpered once more, then fell still.

The whispers of the other entities reverberated

through the rising mist and deep shadows. The language remained unchanged, indecipherable. But she was in tune with all this. The time she and her father spent with the resurrected corpse of Richard—reading the grimoire carved into flaps of his flesh, hearing the explanations from the shredded throat that served as his new mouth—had been time well-spent.

"Father," she said. "Tell them."

"I ..." He coughed. "I offer you blood, spilled in the ring before thousands in attendance ... millions watching from home."

The whispers merged into one voice and spoke words everyone in the room understood.

"In exchange for what, Jack McLaughlin?"

Her father's breath hitched again. Something was stopping him from asking for what he wanted. He stammered and cleared his throat.

"Don't back out now, Daddy," she said. "Ask them."

Through the fog, she saw him stand up straighter and square his shoulders.

Then, he asked them to make him a king.

After twenty-four grueling, sweat-soaked minutes, the blood ritual masquerading as a submission match ended with a bloodied Redneck Miller passing out in Brian's Dead to Rights leg bar. The move was a variation on the Texas Cloverleaf. Brain always made it look snug and painful. Miller was bleeding like a stuck pig in the middle of the ring, his face reduced to a crimson mask. Dead to Rights, indeed. Watching the close-up on his bloody countenance, Jack McLaughlin could hear him scream, even with the sound turned down. Miller's face, contorted in agony, would become an iconic image: a hyper-sigil to carry All-American Professional Wrestling into the apocalyptic new millennium.

Both men had battered each other inside and outside the ring. They'd used steel chairs, the timekeeper's bell, and good old-fashioned fisticuffs. With Brian calling the action, it looked every bit as real as the martial arts exhibitions on the other channel, a far cry from the sports entertainment on the rest of the card or the colorful pageantry of decades past.

Rather than tapping out or crying uncle, Miller lost consciousness. It was the perfect way for his character to go out that night, limp in a puddle of blood, his body having surrendered, though *he* never did. His defiance in the face of defeat and all-around toughness had turned him babyface in the eyes of the crowd. Brian attempting to further pick apart Miller's unconscious body cemented a heel turn months in the making. It was one of those rare moments in the business where everything went according to plan.

Jack embraced his daughter after the whispers went silent and the fog cleared. Reagan squeezed him tightly, knowing she and her father had achieved something special. He'd never been so proud of his daughter. This far surpassed the pride she'd inspired with her cutthroat lemonade operation.

Chip, one of AAPW's investors, lowered his hood and cast Jack a hateful gaze before storming out of the ritual room. He slammed the door on his way out, but it sounded like a cough against the cacophony in Jack's mind. Jack would likely lose Chip as a money mark. That would hurt for a while. Jack hadn't known Chip was Christian. In fact, he seemed to remember Chip having quite an affinity for strippers, particularly ones dangerously close to jailbait age. Jack didn't know much about Jesus, but he was pretty sure such vices were a dealbreaker when it came to a personal relationship with Christ.

"Damn, bro, you think it worked?" D'Amato asked.

McLaughlin looked at the television. Brian was leaving the ring the official victor but no winner in the crowd's eyes. For much of the last decade, he had played the hero. A working-class type with rockstar good looks and an uncanny dedication to in-ring craft who appealed mostly to women, children, and dirt sheet readers. Jack often called him an artist; his canvas was the ring itself, his materials his own body and the bodies of his opponents.

He'd been a loyal soldier, but he'd never drawn the money or mass appeal of Invincible Vincent James, a longtime point of contention between him and Jack. It was something they'd even played up in the build to this heel turn, a simmering bitterness at constantly playing second-fiddle to someone no longer even in the company. Now, he'd fully become the villain, even giving the middle finger to members of the audience. People who'd cheered him for so long now booed him. D'Amato's question circulated in Jack's mind.

Damn, bro, you think it worked?

"We'll have to wait and see," Jack said as he watched Brian, who had helped carry the company during the early-nineties downturn, walk back down the aisle, shoulders stooped.

Jack had no doubts: the ritual *had* worked. This was the dawn of a new era for him and All-American Professional Wrestling. They would once again rise to the top. And this was no deal with the devil, something

McLaughlin would need to pay for with interest at some undetermined later date. With the blood Redneck Miller had spilled in the ring, the balance was paid in full.

After the card ended, the lights came up and the audience cleared out in the usual plodding, frustrated way. Most of the murmurs among them centered on the submission match. Smart marks nerded out over the performances of Brian Hearns and Redneck Miller, while concerned parents bemoaned the bloodshed. Confused children asked some of the same concerned parents if Brian was now a bad guy, never mind that "Bad Guy" had been his moniker for over a decade. They asked why people had cheered Miller. Some guardians stumbled over words as they tried to explain the concept of antiheroes to their impressionable charges. All the outrage, confusion, and enthusiasm crafted the atmosphere necessary for a ritual and one resultant of a ritual.

With the arena emptied, the lights switched off and staff left their stations. The black silence hung in their wake for exactly six minutes before giving way to new light and new voices. The purple fog that had risen from the floor in the ritual room now made walls around the squared circle. The blasphemous whispers rose from it, made loud by their sheer number. They spoke in an inhuman tongue. They spoke in the language of blood.

The blood of Redneck Miller, gone mostly dry or seeped into the mat, came back to life, darkening and liquefying. The crimson puddle bubbled and rippled at the center of the canvas like some vile organism breathed beneath its surface. The canvas itself had changed, its cloth now made of pale, porous flesh slick with feverish sweat, pulsing with uncanny life. A bubble formed on the puddle's surface, swelling tight and cloudy, a murky dome containing the offering, but not for long. When the bubble popped, the blood rose in a pillar. To any human eyes watching, it would've occurred at an excruciatingly slow pace, like video slowed to show every detail. The red tendrils jutted up and up, flecks revolving around them as they knotted to form a thick, bloody rope, a tower of liquid frozen not by cold but by some ungodly gravity.

It rose from the center of the ring, made of so much more substance than what Redneck Miller had visibly spilled to the canvas, not just blood but soul-stuff, which would've remained unseen by the uninitiated. The sanguinary pillar stood thirteen feet. Then it fanned out toward the surrounding purple cloud, blowing out myriad scarlet orbs with pink tails like shooting stars of splatter before disappearing into the violet, hungry murk with a series of thick, gurgling slurps. When the things in the fog had drunk their fill, the fog dissipated, and darkness returned to the arena.

The first to arrive the next morning would find a ring devoid of the blood spilled the previous night. Jack, Reagan, D'Amato, and the others in their inner circle would know the ritual had worked. Their journey toward industry dominance would be well underway.

5

Now —

The vision faded to black, and Brian opened his eyes. Richard's skeleton was sitting atop the black box, one leg crossed over the other and grinning. Sure, skulls were always grinning, but this grin had some feeling behind it, something knowing and smug. Maybe it was the purple glow. The alien light shined in slivers through the gaps between each tooth.

The dissolved parchment had a metallic aftertaste. Brian felt nauseous and woozy. It was one thing to trace the downfall of his career and loss of his rights for over two decades to a strange, bloody, and tragic night. He spent most of those years distrusting what he remembered. As recently as the previous night, it still gave him PTSD episodes. All that was bad enough. Even worse than all that, he'd just learned that the death of Starlite and the appearance of those imps could be traced to the man whose company had given Brian his livelihood. Jack McLaughlin *still* provided occasional financial assistance. All those lawyer fees would've cleared out his savings years ago if not for Jack, and that same resource had been the cause of his troubles from the beginning.

Brian sat and put his face in his hands. Something hard bopped him on the head.

"Hey!" he growled and looked up. The skeleton had smacked him and had reared back for a backhand. It looked goddamned ridiculous and would've made him laugh under other circumstances. "That fucking hurt."

"Good," Richard said, lowering his hand. "I'm here to help, and I can't help you if you're gonna mope."

"Why did Reagan send you if she helped start this shit to begin with?"

Richard held up a finger. "I'm here to help, not to betray my conjurer's confidence."

"Give me a break."

Richard chuckled. Brian looked past him at the black box.

"I was in there a long time. That's why I look the way I do."

"I guess it beats a hole in your throat with flaps of

skin hanging off your body."

"Well, at least now it's somewhat easier to pass along instructions to would-be occultists. Before, they'd read the spell off my skin, but I'd need to provide the color commentary so they understood. With you, though … Well, I trust you *saw* what you had to do."

"I did?"

The skeleton groaned with annoyance. "The circle, the chanting, the blood."

Images of the ritual room floated back to Brian. He saw the symbol Jack's righthand man had drawn on the floor. Heard the chanted words. Saw purple mist. Scarlet blood, first pouring onto the canvas, then rising as a sanguinary pillar of sacrifice.

"I can do it alone? Jack and Reagan had a group with them."

"Sure, more people would equate to more energy, but the engine is already primed. So much blood has fallen over the decades. Your hand in that initial ritual, though unknowing, can command more power than you may know. While the others chanted and asked for things, *you* spilled Redneck Miller's blood. You fed the Agents from your hand."

Heat flared in Brian's cheeks. Screams filled his head. They seemed to come from somewhere in the room. He glanced around, expecting to see her, dogpiled by imps, a pool of her blood spreading across the hardwood. He and Richard were alone.

"Then why did they kill Starlite?" he asked. "They got what they wanted and used me to get it. Why did she have to pay the price?"

Richard didn't answer at first. Perhaps he was considering the question, but without flesh, he made no readable expression. Finally, he said, "A ritual with such large implications comes with great sacrifice. As Agents of change, the creatures you saw only carried out what they deemed necessary."

"But why her? And why *me* if I helped set it all in motion?"

"I wish I knew, but it's beyond our understanding of good and evil," Richard said, sounding defeated.

Brian didn't buy it for a second, but he doubted he'd get anywhere if he pressed him further on the matter.

Something else occurred to him.

"What about this one?" Brian asked. "I can't imagine turning back time is a small feat."

"It's not unlikely that this will carry a heavy price, but just think. You get to go back twenty-five years. You'll still have a wife. A daughter who worships you. A whole career ahead of you. Can any price be too high?"

Brian considered this. He remembered dancing with Melissa at the Broken Spoke in Austin, the way they stumbled over each other's feet and laughed. Her inability to find rhythm never stopped her from dancing to the house songs like Alannah Myles's "Black Velvet" and "Drive" by The Cars. She'd always sing along too, usually almost painfully off-key. He remembered how they used to make love. She'd get all sweaty, hair plastered to the sides of her face, and look down at him with a hungry expression, telling him over and over how good he felt. He remembered how good it felt when they were together.

Unable to handle his always being on the road, she'd divorced him in '95. Genevieve was three at the time. For those first two years, Melissa sent photos of their daughter as she grew. The photos stopped coming after he got locked up. He didn't even get to see her start kindergarten. Melissa hadn't believed that his dalliances with ring rats and ladies of the night didn't start until after they'd separated. She still didn't, as far as he knew, and she never forgave him these transgressions, real and imagined.

And then, there was the career. No matter what he'd believed at the time or what those around him believed, he still had plenty left in the tank before prison. He'd only needed the opportunity to show the world, to show Jack, to show himself.

You get to go back twenty-five years.

Can any price be too high?

The answer was an emphatic *no*.

"You've made your point," he said. "Let's get started."

The purple light brightened behind the skeleton's teeth and inside its eye sockets.

"Excellent," Richard said. "Let's get started."

Brian made space on the living room floor by moving the sofa back and pushing aside the coffee table. He made a large circle using some table salt he'd found in the pantry. In the center, he used some chalk he found in Richard's box to draw the symbol from his vision. He visualized it perfectly. He was no visual artist, but he took his time making every angle, hook, and spiral. Then he lit some candles and set them in the pattern he'd witnessed in the ritual room with Jack and the others. All through the process, Richard looked on, grinning that skeleton grin, unable to make any other expression. The glow in his eyes and behind his teeth dimmed but didn't fade.

Once the setup was finished, Brian grabbed a knife from a rack in the kitchen. When he came back into the living room wielding it, Richard laughed. Brian looked from the skeleton to the knife and frowned.

"What's so damn funny?"

"You're making a blood offering, not committing hara-kiri."

"So, what do I do?"

"A bladejob. Just like you did Redneck Miller. Just like you've done to yourself on numerous occasions."

Brian's knife-free hand went to his forehead, feeling the bumps of blading scars. The sensation made him nostalgic.

"All right," he said, heading back to the kitchen.

He checked some drawers until he found a razorblade. He snapped off a shard and returned to the living room, pinching it between his fingers.

"Got it?" Richard asked. Brian held up the piece. Dull as it was, it still glistened in the light coming through the living room windows. Richard clapped his skeleton hands, and it made a sound like spilled marbles. "Barely a sliver. Good, good. You haven't lost a step, old man."

"Great, so what now?" he asked, ignoring the

backhanded compliment.

Richard gestured toward the circle. "Now you step inside and make your offering."

"Just like that?"

"Just like that."

Brian entered the circle, sliver in hand. He chanted the words he'd overheard in the ritual room. He had no idea what the names meant or their language of origin or how he managed to remember them. He only knew that the words summoned the Agents. These were the same Agents who'd spilled Starlite's blood, and here he was, asking for their help. He chanted and reminded himself that they were neither good nor evil, only Agents of change, moved only by ritual and the intent of others, sustained by the spillage of blood.

The house darkened. Even the outside darkened, though it was barely noon. Brian got the feeling that the house and everyone inside had transported somewhere outside time, somewhere it was always night. It didn't seem far-fetched at all. Nothing seemed unbelievable anymore.

The purple mist rose from the floor, seeped from the shadows on the wall, and lowered from the ceiling. It clouded the darkness and carried the same light that glowed within the skeleton. It looked as though Brian had fallen into a nebula. He could still feel the floor under his feet, but he couldn't see it, and fear it would give way surged within him. It was cold here too, the sort of bone-deep chill that only came on winter days when he'd braved the elements wearing only a light sweater.

He shut his eyes and continued chanting, ignoring the discomfort, ignoring the urge to blow out the candles and run from the house. He could even run all the way back to prison and ask them to lock him up for good. But he stayed inside the circle. It was too late to turn back now. If he somehow found the door through this purple mist and ran outside, would he even want to be where he wound up?

The chanted words continued from his subconscious, a free-flowing stream of strange syllables. Something tingled up and down his legs. Voices spoke from the mist in the same dead language he uttered. Hearing it turned his arms into fields of gooseflesh. Their voices were oppressive, all around like crickets in the woods at night.

"Tell them," Richard said, his voice scraping through the wall of whispers.

Brian cleared his throat. "I offer you blood, spilled in my home."

The whispers merged into one voice and spoke words Brian understood.

"In exchange for what, Brian Hearns?"

Unlike Jack McLaughlin, Brian didn't hesitate.

He asked for a second chance.

Then, he cut into his forehead. The pain was exquisite and familiar. It nearly made him weep but not from discomfort, only from wistful longing as blood and soul stuff drizzled to the floor.

6

The New Before—

Reagan McLaughlin switched off the headlights of her Cadillac Deville and drove under the metal arch at the cemetery where they'd buried Richard Kyle. The black iron fence around the necropolis was hardly visible under the cover of night. She drove without music. The hum of her engine was the only sound. Combined with its raven-black paintjob, the quiet ride made for the discrete approach she needed. Even with the lights in the windows of nearby houses out, she'd need to be quick, which wouldn't be a problem. The funeral had only been that afternoon, and the soil would still be loose. That was good; her dead boyfriend had a lot to answer for.

She parked beside the row where he lay and cut

the engine. When she got out, a chill breeze breathed against her face, making her eyes water. She glanced around for any sign of the caretaker or anyone else who might be spying on her. Though she couldn't see far in the dark, anyone who might be watching probably couldn't either. Satisfied, she went around back and opened the trunk. She glanced around once more before she reached inside and pulled out the spade and a pair of gloves.

Only moonlight guided her as she walked down the row, counting tombstones. Richard's marker was not yet a tombstone but a small plastic sign. His full name, the words *Beloved Son*, and the dates March 16, 1977 to November 23, 1996 were printed on it in black, generic font. She would have missed it were she not actively searching for it.

A mound of fresh dirt covered his burial spot. It was dark and stood stark against the surrounding grass. It had an earthy scent and made a hushed scrape when Reagan plunged the spade into it. Her muscles flared as she lifted the first shovelful and tossed it aside. She repeated the process, her breathing growing heavier and harsher, until sweat soaked her undershirt and pants. When she brushed the last of the earth off the coffin lid, the moon cast a bright, ghostly reflection on the smooth surface that contrasted with her shadow. Reagan sat on the pile she'd made and tried to catch her breath. The air felt colder as it gusted down her throat, harsher. All her muscles felt like they were on fire, especially her arms. It almost made her wish she hadn't come alone.

As her breathing returned to normal, she looked around again to ensure she was unobserved. Then she stood and grabbed the spade. With a heave and a grunt, she jammed its blade under the coffin lid. She leaned all her weight on the handle and tried to pry open the lid. The spade popped out of where she'd lodged it, flipped, and nearly smacked her in the face. She stumbled and spat out a curse.

The moon-bathed grounds lay unchanged around her. The sky and windows of surrounding homes remained dark. No one had taken note of her late-night foray, unless they, too, were hiding, calling the police from the safety of their dark house. She pushed the thought away and snatched the spade back.

Reagan rammed the tool back between the coffin's lid and its base. She leaned on the handle once again, groaning deep in her throat and biting her bottom lip until she tasted blood. The lid splintered and gave with a series of jingles and cracks. It moaned open on its tight hinges and revealed the corpse of Richard.

The mortician had done his best, but it wasn't enough. Reagan wondered if the mortician had known when he finished that he'd failed not from a lack of skill or effort but from a body too ruined to repair. No wonder it'd been a closed casket affair.

Though the hole in Richard's throat had been stitched shut, the ragged edges of the stitching stuck out, even under mere moonlight. And speaking of the moon, his bloodless face matched the hue of the satellite's surface. He'd died from blood loss. How much blood did one need to lose to lose their life? Perhaps she'd ask him when he returned.

Reagan set the spade aside and knelt next to the open grave. She stared down at her lover's eyelids and imagined them opening. She pictured their color and size, their common expression—a faraway, devil-may-care look that had drawn her to him almost instantly. She spoke a series of words in a language forgotten by most. Then she said, "Richard. Richard Kyle. Wake. Up." She slipped into the strange tongue again, loud enough for the right ears to hear but quiet enough not to wake the neighbors. "Richard. Richard Kyle. Wake. Up. There are things I wish to know. Power I wish to wield. You have passed beyond the veil and now must be my teacher. Richard Kyle. Wake. Up."

She never stopped staring at him. She said the words, both the dead ones and the live ones, just as she'd been taught them by Richard himself. The hour was right. Despite all this, his eyes would not open for her.

Something bitter played on her tongue. Her cheeks got hot, and her chest got tight. She felt like cursing the dead man and using the spade to dismember his remains. She almost wanted to leave him unburied and exposed to the elements, then drive back to her dorm and forget this moonlight excursion ever took place.

Almost. Giving up wasn't her style. Never had been, never would be.

She took a breath and gazed back at the dead man's closed eyes. She imagined them opening, showing her his cool expression. She spoke the esoteric words again, slower this time, enunciating more firmly.

"Richard. Richard Kyle. Wake. The fuck. Up." She thought his jaw clenched, but in the shadows, she couldn't be sure. Even still, she felt the butterflies of anticipation. "There are things I wish to know. Power I wish to wield. You have passed beyond the veil and now must be my teacher. Richard Kyle. Wake. Up."

The eyelids twitched and shuddered open. His eyes were cloudier than she remembered. They weren't quite zombielike cataracts. These clouds held a faint color, a faded purple hue. Richard grinned when he spotted Reagan.

"Well, shit," he said in a voice like wet sandpaper. He sat up in the coffin and surveyed their surroundings. Then he faced her. "Aren't you a sight for these dead eyes? I'd say I missed you, but I get the feeling I wasn't gone that long. And honestly? I hardly thought of you at all."

He cackled at his own joke. Reagan stared without humor.

"What?" Richard asked. "It's true. I didn't think of anything. It's called the *void* for a reason."

"So, what? No afterlife?" She kept her tone chilly.

"Oh, please, Reagan. You didn't wake me up to ask me that."

"No," she said. "I want to know what went wrong. You seemed so sure of yourself."

"Maybe a little too sure of myself, unfortunately."

"I conjured you back. I'd appreciate it if you answered me directly." He laughed, and she imagined maggots filled his throat, squirming against each other in an ugly dance routine, a dance of death. She swallowed, and the dryness of her own throat helped her blink away the troubling image. "Why did you fail?"

"I was sloshed when I did the ritual. I didn't ask for the right things. Too sure of myself, like I said. The wording ... it matters."

Reagan McLaughlin laughed so hard she nearly choked. "Of course, you got too trashed to perform the ritual correctly. I should've fucking known."

"I'm glad you're amused."

"What do you care? Seems like it turned out okay for you. Yeah, you're dead, but you don't make it sound so bad."

"It wasn't ... until *somebody* woke me."

"Hey, at least you get another shot at life."

Richard patted himself down, lingering on the poorly stitched hole in his neck. The edges of it pulsed with each undead breath, spaces between each stitch opening like mouths. He glanced at his pale hands, down at the suit they'd dressed him in for burial.

"I would hardly call this life," he said. "You conjured me, which makes me your bitch." At this, Reagan snickered. Richard continued, "Worse still, I can feel myself rotting. Before, I was blissfully unaware. Worst of all, well, how do I say it? It's hard to explain, but once you've been to the void, it's hard to come back. I guess it's like spending the night high on great drugs and sobering up the next day. Not that you'd know anything about that."

"Richard," Reagan said, keeping her voice level, doing everything she could to compose herself in the face of this ridiculous situation. "I'm really sorry you fucked up and died for it."

She hardly got the sentence out before she laughed again. Richard folded his arms and tapped his foot, watching and waiting until she finished. When the last of her cackles died out, he cocked an eyebrow with what looked like great effort.

"Done?" he asked.

"I'm sorry. It's just, well, I didn't expect this to work. I've never spoken to a corpse before. It's all kind of crazy."

"I'm glad I can still amuse you."

"Richard, you will never not amuse me."

"So, that's it then? You called me back from the dead for a laugh? You really are your father's daughter."

All her humor left in a flash. "Let's make that the last time you *ever* compare me to him."

"Aren't we touchy?" He scratched at the stitching in his neck. A thin, green strand of fluid drizzled down the side of his Adam's apple and soaked into his collar. "So, if not for a laugh, why?"

In another future, a future undone, she would've

told him she wanted to know the secret, the way to use blood sacrifice and black magic to achieve one's loftiest goals. She would've gleaned this information from him and shared it with her father, Jack McLaughlin, and helped launch his company, All-American Professional Wrestling, into the stratosphere. She *had* done that very thing, she knew, in a timeline now undone. She knew it in a subtle way, the way she knew her thoughts came from her brain, the way she knew her foot would touch solid ground if she took a step, the way she knew how to breathe. All this had happened—somewhere, sometime—and it also hadn't, which sounded impossible, but she *knew*.

She'd even come here to do that again or for the first time or for the last time.

But this time, her eyes welled up and her bottom lip trembled. These were unfamiliar sensations; Reagan McLaughlin hadn't cried since she was very little. Yet, the tears came now, and she swallowed a sob that threatened to burst out of her. A part of her died as she stood in front of her undead boyfriend in the dark graveyard. It was an ugly part of her, one that didn't care who she hurt as she chased riches and fame. As it died, something else grew in its place, something that would not allow her to set such a harmful series of events in motion.

Reagan McLaughlin wiped her eyes and said something she never said.

She said, "I'm sorry."

7

Someone knocked on the locker room door as the last of Brian Hearns's future memories dissolved. He and Redneck Miller looked at the door. Several seconds passed where Brian lost his train of thought and sense of place. He almost asked Miller what they were talking about and, more embarrassing, where they were, but Miller stood.

"I got it," he said.

As Miller walked to the door, the details of the present scene recalibrated. It was March 23, 1997, the night of *Superslam 13*. Brian and Redneck Miller were going over the details of their match. They'd just discussed doing a spot outside where Brian would attempt to piledrive Miller on the concrete floor. Miller would counter with a back body-drop. It'd be out in the audience. It'd be fucking killer.

Brian started lacing his boots while Miller opened the door.

"Can I come in?" Jack McLaughlin asked.

"You're the boss," Miller said, standing aside.

Brian didn't stop lacing his boots until Jack approached and stood over him.

"How're we doing, boys?" Jack asked.

"Upright and breathing," Miller said.

"Just going over everything," Brian said.

He got a flash of déjà vu when he said those words. He'd said them to Jack many times in the past, sure, but this—the positioning of the men in the room, the actual words, the date, and place—felt especially familiar, which was, of course, impossible. He shook the notion away and went back to work on his boots.

"Right. And it's all coming together?" Jack asked.

"You can trust me," Brian said.

Jack looked at Miller, who only nodded. Again, the flash of déjà vu circulated through him. He knew this had all happened before.

Probably a dream, he thought, and the notion faded again, the way dreams do.

"Now, listen, guys, I want Miller to get some color tonight." Brian stared at Jack. Miller did likewise.

All-American Professional Wrestling had a strict "no juicing" policy. Blood was simply not allowed. It could land them in trouble with their sponsors. "Yeah, I know we have our rules, but I'm asking you to break them. They're my rules, so I trust this won't be a problem."

"Are you sure?" Miller asked, questioning but firm.

"I mean, it will help make him look tougher," Brian said, nodding at Miller, ignoring the feeling that he'd said this before, would say it again, was saying it for the first and last time. "That's what we want, isn't it?"

"Exactly," Jack said, grinning like a carnie who'd found an easy mark.

"One problem," Miller said.

Brian and Jack looked at him. The silence that fell on the room lasted long enough to make Brian fidget.

"Well, what is it, pal?" Jack asked.

"Never done it before," Miller said.

Now Jack looked at Brian. His eyes told Brian he wanted a solution. Brian could offer to cut Miller. He knew how to do it safely and make it look good. Something held him back from voicing this. It pinched his lips shut, kept the words stuffed down somewhere deep. He grimaced and shook his head.

"Not sure what to do, boss. Guess it's not meant to be."

Jack clenched his jaw and eyed Brian a second longer. It was like he felt what Brian felt: that something was off, something he couldn't put his finger on, except to say that something different was supposed to have happened. He turned to Miller and gave the Texan a once-over. Brian's body tensed with anticipation. He didn't know why, but the choice not to cut Miller himself seemed of grave, albeit vague, importance. Something heavy hinged on his refusal. Though he'd never had a problem with getting color to heighten drama, it felt wrong here for reasons he couldn't put into words.

"Shit, I don't know what to tell you," Miller said. "Unless someone wants to give me a blading crash course."

"That won't be necessary," Jack said, but he sounded deflated, even defeated.

Brian brightened when the promoter left.

"It's gonna be a hell of a match," he said.

Miller gave him a single sharp nod, and they resumed going over the spots.

Jack McLaughlin burst into what passed as his office in the Springtown Horizon. The door banged open, and he stomped inside as it wheezed shut behind him. He came to a halt in the center of the room and balled his fists.

The suite was a small cinderblock room with a desk, a sofa, a minifridge full of electrolyte-infused water and bottled protein drinks, and a TV monitor for watching the event taking place in the arena. It smelled like spilled plant soil and rotting meat. The undead Richard Kyle lounged in the office chair with his grave-mud-crusted feet up on the desk and an expectant look in his cloudy eyes.

"I don't know what you're so excited about," Jack said. "They said they're not gonna do it. No blood, no action. The ritual won't work."

Richard remained seated with his expression unchanged. Jack wanted to hit him in his rotting mouth.

"What makes you think there won't be blood tonight?" Richard asked.

Richard, the dead man, had come to Jack himself. Reagan had done a bang-up job awakening him, but not such a good job putting him back down. Her mental state the night she raised him had shifted for the worse in the middle of their graveside conversation, and she'd botched the banishing ritual in spectacular fashion. Like a scorned lover, the undead Richard Kyle hadn't taken too kindly to the half-assed expulsion. Something about existing in two worlds at once was hard on a soul.

He'd come to Jack promising industry dominance, even said that in another timeline, it had already happened, but a guilt-stricken Reagan and a desperate Brian Hearns had seen to its undoing. Richard had come to set things back on track, but if Miller didn't bleed in his match with Brian, it would all be for nothing.

"What are you talking about?" Jack grumbled. "Miller's never bladed before, and Brian offered me no alternative, so we had to put a pin in the idea."

Richard still didn't move from his spot in Jack's chair. He wasn't looking so good these days. Decay had set in. His skin had gone mostly gray with patches of yellow. He'd lost an ear, and maggots were writhing in the hole it left. His nose had sunk into his nasal cavity, its cartilage now no more than a deflated membrane full of snot and death jelly. The stitches in his throat had torn out, opening a ragged hole in his neck. The meat and bone inside undulated when he spoke, and Jack tried his damnedest not to stare, but even a few months after their initial meeting, he couldn't help himself. It drew the eye the way exhibits in a museum of medical oddities might.

Richard Kyle looked like absolute shit, but he shook

his head and laughed.

"What's so goddamn funny?" Jack asked, tightening his fists.

"You really don't know anything, do you?"

Jack's chest tightened. He took a breath that felt laborious and fixed Richard with a glare.

"Richard, so help me God, if you don't shoot straight with me, I will find a way to put you under ground forever. Or maybe I'll just have you dismembered and buried alive. Or undead. Whatever the hell you are. And I'll scatter the pieces in different parts of the world, so you won't be able to put your miserable, rotting ass back together again."

Richard's expression lost all humor.

"The plan will still unfold, McLaughlin." His eyes glowed deep purple. "There will be some differences, sure, but there *will* be a sacrifice tonight. It won't mean a thing, though, unless you get your ass to the ritual room on the double. You know the others can't do a damn thing without you."

"Are you giving me orders now?"

"Only advice," Richard said. "Miller will bleed tonight. You get to decide if it means anything."

8

Brian came through the curtain to make his entrance. Miller paced the ring like a starving panther in a zoo cage. The audience swelled with a mix of cheers and boos. He'd nixed the spillage of blood, but the planned double turn would move forward. By the end of this bout, people would cheer Miller and boo Brian. But no blood. Brian couldn't quite articulate why that was important now, but he knew. Instincts were important, and his instincts told him blood tonight, especially if spilled by his hand, would be bad.

Brian came through the ropes, and Miller tackled him with the force of a double-decker bus hitting an unfortunate cyclist. There was no chance for the ref to go over the rules, no chance for a stare-down before the bell. It rang a half-second after the men collided, signaling the start of a war already underway.

Brian and Miller spilled out of the ring nearly right away, exchanging blows that drew shocked expressions from the audience and the ref. It had the look and feel of an actual fight, the sort of reality-based work that Brian prided himself on. They took turns battering each other with fists and kicks. Brian fought through more feelings of déjà vu. He wondered if Miller was doing the same.

Miller hurled Brian back-first into the barricade. Brian backdropped Miller onto the concrete. Each high-impact throw sent waves of pain through the competitors, but this was satisfying pain, the pain that came from hard work, the pleasant aches of giving one's all.

After backdropping Miller, Brian stomped on the inside of Miller's right knee. Miller cried out like a wounded beast, selling the move like a pro. When they got back in the ring, Brian chop-blocked Miller's same knee and wrapped it around the ring post. Once. Twice. Three times. It looked real as hell, but Miller hardly felt a thing.

The art of this came down to hurting one another without injuring one another. It was illusionism, magic, but still physical. A seemingly spent Miller hugged the corner of the ring, his legs draped to the outside. He grimaced with put-on pain and tried to catch his breath as Brian searched around the ring for a weapon. First, he snatched the bell from ringside and tossed it on the ring apron. Next, he grabbed a steel chair and reentered the ring.

Miller crawled across the canvas, struggling to regain a vertical base. Brian stalked him like a shark stalking prey. He waited for Miller to get in a wobbly stance and chop-blocked him again, this time using the edge of the chair. Miller groaned in agony and crumbled back to the canvas. Brian opened the chair enough to slide Miller's apparently injured right leg through it. He stomped on the chair, closing it hard around Miller's already aching tendons. Miller flailed and screamed, and Brian stomped the chair again. Miller lay flat on his back, wincing and gasping for air.

With his opponent prone, Brian climbed the corner to the second rope, setting his sights on the leg trapped in the chair. This was a tried-and-true spot, made to look like a worker had broken his opponent's ankle. It was good for when someone needed to take some time off to heal nagging injuries. A believable-looking worked injury angle was an effective way to get someone off TV for the necessary amount of time. Brian prepared to leap.

Sensing his peril, Miller rolled out of the way and kicked the chair loose. Brian landed and tried to get his bearings, but Miller waffled him across the back with the chair. Brian yelled and sank to his knees. Miller whacked Brian across the back again, and the audience lost their shit, screaming like rabid Romans at the coliseum as lions took down a one-time favorite but now overexposed gladiator.

Miller grabbed Brian's legs and tried to twist them into Brian's very own Dead to Rights submission hold. Brian jabbed a thumb into Miller's eye, freeing himself from the hold. He stood and tried to tackle Miller, but Miller sidestepped, and Brian sailed through the ropes, landing on the floor.

If Brian had chosen to cut Miller or if Miller had known how to blade, now would've been a good spot to do it. They were in the middle of this hotly contested match. The action had spilled outside for the second time. It had already been intense, but blood would push this bout to an even more feverish level. Plus, it would make the ending mean more, make it look even more like Miller was fighting from underneath. He'd look simultaneously tougher and more sympathetic. But there'd be no blood. Blood was bad. He didn't know why, only that it was.

Miller grabbed Brian by the arm and went to whip him into the steel barricade. Brian reversed the throw, tossing Miller there instead. Miller shot in low, driving his own head into the steel. The blood came almost instantly. He'd busted himself open hardway. Something heavy and acidic sunk into the pit of Brian's stomach, and for a handful of seconds, he stood and stared at his battered, bleeding opponent. Time itself slowed to a crawl. The cacophony of the crowd warped, muffled by the blood pounding in Brian's veins.

They couldn't just stop the match. They needed to go through it.

As Brian tromped over and grabbed Miller by the blood-soaked hair, he told himself it'd all be fine. A little blood would heighten the match's drama. Why had he been so afraid to spill it himself? And since *he* hadn't done the cutting, maybe it would all be okay.

As he dragged Miller back to the ring, the crowd roared for the wounded Redneck to hang on and fight through the pain. Brian grabbed the chair from earlier and drove it over and over into Miller's knee. He pulled the blows a fraction of an inch away from the flesh. It looked vicious, and the audience lapped it up. The air thrummed with their fervor. Blood spattered the canvas, turning seemingly everything red. Every streak and puddle looked like a sigil painted by a mad magician. Brian did his best to ignore the patterns, the awful notion that the metaphor his mind conjured was not far off. He had a match to finish, and he fought through the dread.

Brian rammed Miller into the corner and attempted wrapping the injured leg in the ropes. Miller shoved him back and kicked him in the nuts. With a cry of pain, Brian fell backwards, holding his family jewels. Above him, the blinding lights reminded him of a UFO, hovering moments before he levitated into the guts of the vessel.

Brian tried to crawl to the ropes on the side of the ring where he'd stashed the bell while Miller struggled to his feet in the corner. Miller got up first and climbed atop Brian's back to lock in a choke. The audience noise vibrated everything around them. The air, the canvas, the ropes: it all shook with unbridled, bloodthirsty energy. They wanted to see Brian Hearns tap out. They wanted to see him fight back and vanquish his longtime foe. They were completely torn, but regardless of where any of them stood, they were all in the palms of the performers' hands.

Brian grabbed the plywood-backed bell and swung it backwards over his head. It connected with Miller's skull, making a resounding ding. Miller released the choke and fell semiconscious to the center of the ring.

Brian stood, soaked in sweat and some of Miller's blood, and tossed the bell aside. He turned to face his fallen opponent, grabbed the bleeding man's legs, and twisted him into Dead to Rights. Blood ran from Miller's forehead, soaking his hair, spilling down the front of his face, drizzling into a puddle on the mat. He groaned and tried to press his way out of the hold, but Brian held on, laying all his weight into it. Eventually, Miller passed out in the hold, but he never verbally surrendered. That was important for the audience to remember. It showed Miller had the heart of a champion.

The bell rang, and the ref raised Brian's hand. Brian shook the ref off and went back on the attack, even though he'd won, even though Miller wasn't conscious. Several more officials came to pry him away. The audience bombarded him with boos, but he smiled on the inside. It was a hell of a performance, and the blood had heightened the drama. He hadn't spilled it himself; Miller had gotten color on his own. Brian's conscience was clear.

After the card ended, the lights came up and the audience cleared out in the usual plodding, frustrated way. Most of the murmurs among them centered on the submission match. Smart marks nerded out over the performances of Brian Hearns and Redneck Miller, while concerned parents bemoaned the bloodshed. Confused children asked some of the same concerned parents if Brian Hearns was now a bad guy. They asked why people had cheered Miller. Some guardians stumbled over words as they tried to explain the concept of antiheroes to their impressionable charges. All the outrage, confusion, and enthusiasm crafted the atmosphere necessary for a ritual and one resultant of a ritual.

With the arena emptied, the lights switched off and staff left their stations. The black silence hung in their wake for exactly six minutes before giving way to new light and new voices. The purple fog that had risen from the floor in the ritual room now made walls around the squared circle. The blasphemous whispers rose from it, made loud by their sheer number. They spoke in an inhuman tongue. They spoke in the language of blood.

The blood of Redneck Miller, gone mostly dry or seeped into the mat, came back to life, darkening and liquefying. The crimson puddle bubbled and rippled at the center of the canvas like some vile organism breathed beneath its surface. The canvas itself had changed, its cloth now made of pale, porous flesh slick with feverish sweat, pulsing with uncanny life. A bubble formed on the puddle's surface, swelling tight and cloudy, a murky dome containing the offering but not for long. When the bubble popped, the blood rose in a pillar. To any human eyes watching, it would've occurred at an excruciatingly slow pace, like video slowed to show every detail. The red tendrils jutted up and up, flecks revolving around them as they knotted to form a thick, bloody rope, a tower of liquid frozen not by cold but by some ungodly gravity.

It stood at the center of the ring, made of so much more substance than what Redneck Miller had visibly spilled to the canvas, not just blood but soul-stuff, which would've remained unseen by the uninitiated. The sanguinary pillar stood thirteen feet. Then it fanned out toward the surrounding purple cloud, blowing out myriad scarlet orbs with pink tails like shooting stars of splatter before disappearing into the violet, hungry murk with a series of thick, gurgling slurps. When the things in the fog had drunk their fill, the fog dissipated, and darkness returned to the arena.

The first to arrive the next morning would find a

ring devoid of the blood spilled the previous night. Jack and the others in his inner circle would know the ritual had worked. Their journey toward industry dominance would be well underway. Again.

9

When Brian Hearns got to his hotel room after the knock-down, drag-out battle with Redneck Miller, he took his address book out of his luggage. He paged to the S-section and found Starlite's name and number. He got as far as picking up the phone on the nightstand, but before he could dial his Chicago girl, he hung up and closed the book. Images burbled from the ether of his subconscious of blood and clawed hands. Someone nearby was screaming. No, not nearby but inside his head.

The imagery and sounds tore through him. His already aching muscles went painfully tense. Every breath came in short and sharp, never feeling like he'd gulped enough air. He sat on the bed, unable to move. The screams sounded closer and outside his body. The creatures with clawed hands would soon follow, scrambling over the bedclothes to come and chew out Brian's eyes and throat. It felt beyond dream, beyond memory, almost as if it were happening now.

He and Starlite were in bed. She was sitting on his face.

Then those things came out of the wall. He stood there helpless as they ripped into her.

Imps, he thought. *Agents.*

All of that had happened, and yet it hadn't.

His head swam with woozy confusion. He'd felt disoriented all goddamn night and just wanted this all to end, whatever all this was.

It happened here in this room. They came out of the wall above the headboard.

It happened, happens, will happen tonight.

He pressed his hands into his temples and leaned back on the bed.

I wish I knew why I feel so uneasy.

Because you tampered with reality, a voice he recognized but didn't recognize spoke up.

You fucked with the timeline, and now you're paying the price.

None of that made any sense to him, so he had room service bring him a couple bottles of whiskey and set about drinking away his troubles. Even as inebriation set in and he relaxed, he put his address book back in his suitcase. He wouldn't be calling his Chicago girl or any girl tonight. Something told him it was important that he didn't. It was the same something that told him not to volunteer to cut Miller's head. The same something that had given him these bizarre, troubling images, scenes that couldn't have been dream or memory but had to have come from somewhere. Perhaps he was losing his mind from too many drops on the head.

That latter notion disturbed him no more or no less than any other crazy idea that slipped through his increasingly intoxicated mind. Halfway through the first bottle, all the worries had drowned and only sleep concerned him. When he crashed, he crashed hard. Mercifully, he had no dreams.

When he woke the next morning, Brian Hearns called home. Melissa answered and asked if he wanted to talk to their daughter, Genevieve. Her voice sounded startled. It almost always did in the days since their divorce. She seemed not just surprised to hear from him but also scared, as if worried he'd say something she wouldn't want to hear.

"No," he said. "I want to talk to you."

"Oh," she said.

It came out in a nearly breathless croak, as if he had his hand around her throat. He hadn't been a perfect husband, but he never put his hands on her, at least not in an aggressive manner. She never told him why she acted this way, like she was afraid of him. To be fair, he never asked or told her she didn't need to be afraid.

"Yeah, I just …" He paused, not sure how to proceed. He clutched the receiver with one hand and twirled the cord with the other. Melissa didn't interject. She aimed to make him say whatever he hoped to say. The disorientation and near-paralyzing fear from the previous night had faded, along with the frightening hallucinations. Memories of growing old behind bars had mostly gone altogether; when they did surface, they felt like no more than bad dreams. While a hangover now racked his body, throbbing behind his eyes and holding his leg muscles in the grip of dehydration, a strange lucidity had settled over him. More than anything, he felt assured that not spilling Miller's blood himself put him in the clear in case there were any spiritual repercussions. "I just miss you," he said.

"I miss you too." She said it in a whisper.

"You do?"

"Of course," she said.

"I just thought … Is there someone else? Has there been anyone since I moved out?"

"What's bringing this on?" she asked.

In the background, Genevieve giggled and screamed with another child around her age. It brought a smile to Brian's lips. This could be a new beginning, a real new beginning.

"I want to come home. Can I come home?"

"When?" she asked.

"Tonight, after TV. Will you be awake?

"I'll wait up if you want to talk."

"I'll be there," he said. "I swear."

He spent the rest of the day at the gym, thinking about how he would rebuild his life.

After TV, Brian took the first flight from Chicago to Austin. Melissa lived in a house on Lake Travis. They got it after their wedding in 1989. It previously belonged to her parents. Despite being very well-off, her father was a huge wrestling fan and was overjoyed when she announced her engagement to Bad Guy Brian Hearns. Melissa's parents signed the home over to the newlyweds not considering for a second the possibility that their daughter couldn't handle a husband who was always on the road.

Brian took a cab out to his old place and tipped the driver handsomely. When he saw one of the lamps was on inside the house, he breathed a sigh of relief. He'd half-expected her to not wait up for him. Why would she? She'd never been able to before. Why should she start now?

As he walked up to the front door, he wondered, not for the first time, if maybe there was more to their split than his heavy traveling. Not something on her end, such as an affair, but something more he could've done to make his prolonged absences less difficult for her to endure. Sure, he'd asked her this when she first broke the news of wanting a divorce, but she'd already made up her mind, hardened herself to anything he might have said.

That was two years ago, though. Maybe tonight could be different. The fact she'd agreed to let him come over was promising.

He knocked gently and waited. When he heard the door unlocking, his breath caught. He was a high school kid again, coming to pick up his date and nervous as hell.

She opened the door. With the light from the lamp at her back, her face was obscured by shadow. He could make out some of the contours of it as well as eyes like twin dark pools, but otherwise, she was a half-formed image. Only the coconut scent of her shampoo and the way she stood, leaning on one foot behind the other, gave away that it was her.

Brian wrapped her in an embrace. She stepped into him, at first keeping her arms stiff at her sides. Then she squeezed him around his waist. The tightness of her grip and the way she rested her head on his chest showed him she meant what she'd said about missing him. The two years since their last touch seemed like ten times as much time had passed. In a way, it had, though he could no longer explain why. It was like whole chunks of memories were missing, as if he'd lived a whole forgotten lifetime.

That didn't matter, though. Right now mattered. This woman in his arms mattered. Repairing his life mattered. He loosened his hold on her and tilted her face up to meet his.

"Where's Genevieve?" he asked.

"Asleep."

"Asleep," he repeated and slowly moved in for a kiss.

She didn't pull away or resist, though he half-expected she might. She even brought her lips forward those last few inches to meet his. They were every bit as soft as he remembered. On one hand, he couldn't believe his luck. On the other, if coming home had been as easy as giving her some time before simply asking, he was a fucking moron for not asking her sooner. Sure, she could've told him to come home or never divorced him in the first place, but he didn't need to worry about that now. No sense in blaming her or himself or anyone. Only the present moment of reunion was important. Even so, after a few breathless seconds of kissing his former wife, he pulled away and asked a stupid question.

"Why'd you let me come back?" he asked.

He didn't expect an answer, at least not one beyond the already stated, "I miss you."

"Because I dreamed of us," she said, "only I don't think it was a dream. You were in a hotel room with a hooker." The declarative statement made his guts clench, but he didn't stop her. "In my dream, someone killed this woman. You didn't kill her, but everyone thought you did, even me, even Genevieve. You went to prison for over twenty years. I tried marrying again, but it was never the same. Our daughter grew to resent you and resent me, even though neither of us were wrong. You didn't kill anyone, and we were separated when you were with this woman. I did what I thought was right based on the information I had. She hated me, though … Genevieve, I mean … she hated me and told me right to my face more than once. And I hated myself too. In my dream, you had a chance to reset things. All you had to do was offer your blood to these creatures. They were the same creatures that killed that woman, but they also had the power to set things right. And you did. You set things right, and now you're here."

"It sounds like a crazy dream," Brian said, despite a creeping notion that it hadn't been a dream at all. Everything she just laid out had happened. He had changed something, lost something to regain something. He could not acknowledge it, though. It was too unbelievable, despite echoes of dream memories. More so, he didn't *want* to acknowledge it. The sooner he forgot it, the more likely he could get away with it. "I'm glad I'm here," he said with a firmness he hoped would ward off any lingering dread or uncertainty.

"I am too," she said. She took his hand and led him through the door, telling him to come in. "I'm not ready to be with you yet, but we should talk. We need to get to know each other again."

He followed her inside and closed the door. Her words *I'm not ready to be with you yet* brought a pang of regret that he felt mostly in his crotch but also in his heart. They had to find each other's pace, then find one that pleased them both. He vowed to embrace whatever course they landed on, to embrace every moment back with his family, and remember to be grateful. The nightmare future, real or imagined, would not come to pass. He would not let it, and he did his best to ignore images of Miller's blood smeared in occult patterns across his mind's eye.

Melissa made tea while Brian went to Genevieve's room and watched his daughter sleep. She slept in a bigger bed now. Her hair had darkened and grown much longer. She was taller too, and thinner. He ignored the temptation to shake her awake and make sure she still recognized him. Of course she would; only two years had passed, not twenty-five.

Not twenty-five.

Brian and Melissa reconvened on the sofa in the living room. The whole area had a rustic cabin look with its wood paneling and stone fireplace. The rest of the house wasn't much different. It was initially intended as a vacation spot, not a homestead, and when his in-laws gifted them the property, he and Melissa talked extensively about updating the fixtures. It never got past the talking stage, and Brian long suspected

Melissa secretly liked the look of this house. The fact it had retained its cabin by the lake look in the time he'd been gone only proved it. He said as much now, and she laughed.

God, how he missed the sound of her laugh.

"How's Genevieve doing in school?" Brian asked.

"Good. She likes it."

"Does she ever talk about me?"

"Oh, all the time," Melissa said with a wry smile. "She misses her daddy."

"And I miss her. And you."

Melissa gave Brian's hand a light squeeze.

She'd made peppermint tea with a hint of honey, his favorite. Hot as it was, drinking it always made him feel cooler and clearer.

"How do you get this to taste so good?" he asked.

She laughed again. "I just buy the bags from the store."

"I swear you do *something* to it, woman."

She hummed. "Maybe I do. Maybe it's my magic potion, and that's why you're back." The mention of magic made him set the mug down. "What's wrong?" she asked.

"I don't know," he said. "It's … hard to put into words."

"Something about the dream I mentioned?"

He shook his head. "It's more than that, but yeah, that's part of it."

"So, tell me."

He opened his mouth to do just that, fully intending on baring his soul and telling her everything, no matter how outlandish or unbelievable. But before he could get a single syllable out, he saw it—one of those fucking imps, those *Agents*—crawling out of an opening in the wall that hadn't been there seconds before.

"No!" he cried.

Memories of a timeline that should've been erased flooded his brain with terror. Panic flashed across Melissa's face. He reached for her, but the demon was faster. It leapt from the split in the wall and ensnared itself in her hair. Others followed, spilling out like a deluge of muscular babies from a ragged, ruined birth canal. One slammed into his chest, taking the breath out of him and knocking him to his back.

Kill me, he thought. *Not her. Please. Kill me, and let's be done with this.*

Just leave. My family. Alone.

The Agents granted no such wish. One kept him pinned to the floor while the others tore into Melissa with gnashing teeth and raking claws. They tore into her throat, moistening and muffling her screams. They slashed angry, crimson gills into her cheeks. One clawed finger popped her left eye like an overripe grape. Another imp gnawed on her right ear.

Brian tried with every ounce of strength he had to get up, but the creature sitting on his chest possessed uncanny strength. He didn't remember them being this strong. How did he remember them at all? he wondered, knowing that he remembered it because it happened, just as *this* was happening.

This was cruel inevitability. All he had wanted was a second chance, a way to set things right when so much had gone wrong. He should have known better, though. Fate is a stubborn motherfucker, and the past wouldn't let itself be altered so easily.

And what could be a more profound reminder than watching the mother of his child have her face peeled from her skull?

Another scream filled the room.

Genevieve. Dear God, Genevieve!

His daughter stood at the foot of the stairs, watching the horrific sight. Her wails of grief and shock drew the attention of the Agents. They left Melissa twitching in a bloody pool and set their sights on her.

"NO, PLEASE!" Brian cried and redoubled his efforts

to lift the fiend off his chest as the others swarmed after Genevieve, who turned and ran up the stairs.

He rammed fists into the imp's head and body. He squirmed and kicked. Though he was a full two hundred thirty-five pounds, this deceptively small creature kept him pinned. It was emasculating, terrifying, and frustrating all at once. Hot tears spilled down his face. His throat was raw from screaming. Every muscle in his body burned from the struggle. It was a useless struggle, a futile effort.

He did not get up until the imp let him up. But by then, it was too late.

Genevieve was already screaming.

Brian barreled up the stairs. The imp that had held him down stayed behind, laughing at him, at his misfortune, at his tragedy. The laughter was a high-pitched, warbly sound, part child and part wild animal. It filled his head, impossibly loud, a solid, suffocating thing that drowned out the hard and heavy thuds of his feet on the hardwood stairs.

He leapt over the last few steps and bounded down the hall to Genevieve's room.

God, why didn't she run out the front door?

He slammed shoulder-first through the ajar bedroom door. The Agents already had their claws in her. Two of the fuckers held each limb. They had her on the floor, ready to quarter the poor girl. She writhed in their taloned grasp, shrieking and cursing.

Brian got a running start and kicked the nearest two—the ones holding down her left leg. The impact connected, sending painful vibrations up his leg that nearly took him off his feet. By some miracle or the element of surprise, the fiends released her, tumbling ass over teakettle, tangling with each other, and crashing into the nightstand. The lamp tipped and smashed into them, shattering into hundreds of ceramic shards.

The remaining six let her go and set their sights on Brian. Genevieve scrambled to her feet and ran into his arms. He wanted to squeeze her and never let go, but there was no time. The police would be here soon, and no matter what he or Genevieve said about imps or Agents, they would undoubtedly conclude that Brian Hearns had murdered his ex-wife.

He gently but urgently positioned Genevieve behind him and swiped a shard from the floor. He pressed the jagged end against his forehead.

"Dad!" Genevieve yelped.

The Agents bellowed out a collective protest as Brian sliced into his own flesh.

10

Another New Before —

Jack McLaughlin rose from his desk in his office at the Springtown Horizon. The dead man grinned from the chair across from him. His lips had rotted away so much he hardly had to part them to show his mud-crusted teeth. One eye gleamed, while worms writhed in the hole where the other had resided. The way the worms moved, it looked like they, too, were excited for the coming ritual, a ritual that would be set in motion for a third time, though only the Agents knew this consciously. Everyone else, Jack and the undead Richard included, only had vague recollections, like images from a mostly forgotten dream.

It was this odd feeling, begotten by these glimpses of timelines that once were but had now been undone, that made Jack hesitate now.

"What is it?" Richard asked through the hole in his throat.

"Something's wrong," Jack said. "Don't you feel it?"

Richard did, but he couldn't put his finger on just what it was. Even in death, certain details eluded him.

"It will pass," he said. "Do what must be done. After that, the world is at your feet."

Jack gave the dead man a tight-lipped smirk and a curt nod. He stepped around the desk, and the door banged open. Reagan was standing in the frame, pointing a handgun at her father's face. Her expression was cold, as if she somehow knew all the pain that would result from her already powerful father's immersion in dark magic.

"What?" Jack said. "Baby, what—"

She didn't give him a chance to get another word out. She squeezed the trigger, and his face disappeared in a chunky, crimson cloud of gore. He crumpled to the floor, missing the upper half of his head, the last bursts of life spurting from within like a dying fountain. His limbs twitched, not in protest but simply instinct. Jack McLaughlin was dead.

Reagan looked across the corpse of her father at the decaying man who stood opposite her.

Richard grinned again, wider now. The worms in

his eye socket increased the speed of their enthusiastic, anticipatory writhing. She lowered the gun and stepped toward him. Her high heel pierced the palm of her father's hand like a stigmata wound. She reached for Richard with warm hands full of life, and he reached for her with hands room temperature and gray. He was considerably cooler, but she didn't care. She owed everything to him; every version of her, from this timeline to the ones that had been snuffed out through ritual after ritual, knew this fundamentally. They embraced and kissed, his cold tongue like a squirming slab of sushi in her mouth.

Behind them, a new sanguinary pillar rose from the floor where Jack McLaughlin's blood was shed. Too big even for the considerable amount of blood he had lost, it bolstered its growth with soul-stuff, crimson and vital, as purple mist clouded the room, and the Agents once again emerged to feed.

Who is Lucas Mangum?

Award-nominated author of a dozen books, including the Digital Darkness series, Saint Sadist, and Gods of the Dark Web. Vaporwave Dad. You can join his newsletter at:

https://www.lucasmangum.com/

MORE FROM

MADNESS HEART PRESS

Czech Extreme by Edward Lee
isbn: 978-1-955745-06-2

The Television by Edward Lee
isbn: 978-1-955745-28-4

Mania by Lucas Mangum
isbn: 978-1-087893-98-3

Bestial by Lucas Mangum
isbn: 978-1-955745-51-2

Extinction Peak by Lucas Mangum
isbn: 979-8-689548-65-4

You Will Be Consumed by Nikolas Robinson
isbn: 978-1-7348937-7-9

Curse of the Ratman by Jay Wilburn
isbn: 978-1-955745-19-2

Addicted to the Dead by Shane McKenzie
isbn: 978-1-955745-15-4

Muerte con Carne by Shane McKenzie
isbn: 978-1-955745-33-8

CPSIA information can be obtained
at www.ICGtesting.com
Printed in the USA
JSHW080352180723
44886JS00001B/122